Marlowe was o. . . . . Body riddled
with bullets. I'd never liked riddles and now I
knew why. She glanced down at the corpse for
a split second and then lifted her doelike eyes
to mine. As the streetlights shone through her
nightgown I could see the outline of her gams
perfectly. She was one hot potato all right.

She took a couple of steps toward me, walk-
ing over poor dead Marlowe to get there. She
had guts, this dame. So did Marlowe, but his
were all over the floor. She took one step closer
and I could see the heaving of her breasts. If
that wasn't an invitation, I don't know what is.

Hungrily, I took her in my arms and kissed
her roughly. Our mouths came together firmly
like two freight cars coupling at Grand Central.
After a moment, she pulled away from me.

"You think you're pretty tough, doncha?" she
said, ogling my physique.

"I get around on my fists all right," I said.

"That sounds like a pretty clumsy way to get
around," she said seductively. I knew she
wanted me to kiss her again, so I went for her.

The next thing I knew, I was out cold.

ALSO BY THE AUTHOR:

FUTURE MAC SLADE MYSTERIES:

The CASE of the HARDBOILED DICKS

A MAC SLADE MURDER MYSTERY

John Blumenthal

A FIRESIDE BOOK
Published by Simon & Schuster, Inc.
New York

A Fireside Book
Published by Simon & Schuster, Inc.
Simon & Schuster Building
Rockefeller Center
1230 Avenue of the Americas
New York, New York 10020

FIRESIDE and colophon are registered trademarks of
Simon & Schuster, Inc.

Designed by Rueith Ottiger/Levavi & Levavi

Manufactured in the United States of America

1   3   5   7   9   10   8   6   4   2

Library of Congress Cataloging in Publication Data
Blumenthal, John.
The case of the hardboiled Dicks.

"A Fireside book."
I. Title.
PS3552.L8485C3   1985   813'.54   85-2067
ISBN 0-671-55538-3

"Crime doesn't pay."
—J. EDGAR HOOVER

"Wanna bet?"—ROBERT VESCO

A swift kick in the gut is usually all it takes to wake a guy up. That's all it took to wake *me* up, anyway. Offhand, I'd opt for one of those nice digital alarms with snooze control, but that morning I happened to be caught by a copper, napping in the doorway of the Ace Tuxedo Rental Agency at Thirty-third and Third. To add insult to injury, it was one of those female coppers, a meter maid with sharp boots.

I had a feeling it wasn't going to be my day. A gut feeling, you might say.

"Hey, scum," the lady copper said in a voice that sounded like she'd sprinkled gravel on her Raisin Bran that morning.

I looked up at her from the curb, and from that eye-view she looked like King Kong in fuzz blues. "That's *Mr.* Scum to you, sweetheart," I said.

"Don't sweetheart me, dork," she said. She was clever with the repartee, this one. "The sidewalk ain't a hotel."

"Gee, I *thought* the room service was a little on the slow side," I said.

She wasn't amused, so I got to my feet. My whole body was sore, my head was pounding and my tongue felt like high-grade sandpaper. I would've asked the lady copper for an Anacin, but she was fondling her nightstick in a way that was anything but seductive. That kind of painkiller I didn't need.

"I don't wanna see your ugly mug in this neighborhood again," she said. "If I do, you'll wish you was never born."

I took that for a subtle hint to get my butt out of there pronto. Even with a hangover I can be pretty alert. Without further ado, I picked my fedora off the pavement, punched out the dents and doffed it politely at her.

On the way to my office I tried to remember how I'd ended up spending the night on the sidewalk. I've got a notoriously rotten memory, so it all came back to me in bits and pieces. I was on a case, nothing special, just your ordinary divorce job, and I'd been trailing this broad all over the goddamn city. Her husband had hired me to find out if she'd been screwing around with someone. "Someone" was putting it mildly—the dame had a little black book that made the Manhattan phone directory look like light reading.

Anyhow, her poor dumb bastard of a husband had given me this lead—that's what he'd called it, anyway. He'd told me to go to this bar down at Thirty-third and Third and ask the bartender for a guy named Finn. Mickey Finn was the guy's full moniker. The name sounded familiar somehow, but I couldn't place it. So I did like he said—I went to the bar, ordered a Scotch and soda on the rocks and asked the barkeep for this Finn fella. The next thing I knew, everything went blurry on me and I was out cold on the sidewalk. Maybe he'd put something in my drink. I don't know.

It was nine-thirty by the time I'd walked the ten blocks to my office at Forty-second and Lex. My body was still sore as hell and my gut felt like somebody had force-fed me a jar of chili peppers. Since it was Thursday, my gal Friday, Tuesday, wasn't in yet, so I poured myself a cup of java that tasted like something the city uses to fill potholes with, and settled down with my *Racing Form*. I had a feeling it was going to be a slow day.

I was dead wrong. No sooner had I gotten to the first race at Aqueduct than this classy dame comes barreling into my office without so much as a knock on the door. I could tell she was a classy dame because she wasn't chewing gum.

"Are you Mac Slade?" she asked breathlessly. I didn't say anything, but I gave her the once-over by peering over the top edge of my newspaper. She was quite a dish, that's for sure, about five-eight in heels, redheaded and with a build that wouldn't quit, not even on Sundays.

"Who wants to know?" I retorted obtusely, amazed that I could be that suave that early in the morning what with a stomach growling like a caged leopard and a head pounding like a steel-drum recital.

"*I* do, of course," she said. There was a sharp edge to her voice that could have cut through cement. I had the feeling that this dame meant business.

Finally I put the *Racing Form* down and gave her the once-over again, what you might call the twice-over, I guess. The second time was no disappointment either:

she was more than a dish; she was a whole set of china—saucers, gravy boat and all.

"What can I do for you?" I asked, gesturing for her to take a load off her feet, though the load couldn't have been much more than 110 pounds, if you didn't include the five-pound rock on her finger. She hiked her dress up a couple of crucial inches and settled into a chair. There's nothing like a perfect set of gams to get the old ticker cranking in the morning, and she had the best set I'd seen in a month. I didn't want her to catch me ogling them, though, so I ogled her chest instead.

"It's my brother, Link," she said, her bosom still heaving from the twelve-flight schlepp up to my office. "He's been missing for two weeks and . . . I just don't know . . . what to do."

With that, she pulled a lace hanky out of her cleavage and started bawling. Bawling dames drive me crazy, so I did my best to calm her down.

"Well, you came to the right place, lady," I said. "I specialize in missing Links."

But that only made her bawl louder, so I figured I'd better try the sympathetic approach.

"Now, now," I told her in my most sin-

11

cere consoling voice. "There's nothing to worry about, miss. People disappear all the time. According to the latest Justice Department statistics, only ninety-four percent of them turn up dead."

For some reason, the sympathetic approach didn't make her feel any better, either. She was bawling like a banshee now. I didn't know what else to say, so I watched her crying her eyes out for about three minutes, then I did the daily crossword, checked the want ads and read the sports section cover to cover. The Mets weren't doing too hot as usual and the Yankees had lost their star pinch-hitter to Cleveland. It must've been a good twenty minutes before she quit with the melodramatics.

"I'm terribly sorry," she said, wringing her sopping handkerchief out on the two-month old salami sandwich that had bonded itself to my desk blotter. "I don't know what came over me. You must think I'm an awful silly goose."

"Don't worry about it," I said. "I get a lot of geese up here in my office, silly and otherwise." I figured a little attempt at humor might cheer her up, but it didn't. "Now why don't you just tell me all about your brother, Miss . . ."

"Smith," she said, right on cue. "Mary Smith. And it's not Miss. It's Ms."

Oh boy, a feminist dame, I thought to myself. Just what I needed. First a lady copper with happy feet, now a feminist dame. Just between you and me, I need feminist dames like a moose needs a hat rack.

Anyhow, this Smith dame dabbed the last teardrops off her gorgeous kisser and launched into a spiel about her missing brother. Something about it sounded rehearsed, don't ask me why. Maybe it was because she was reading it off a stack of three-by-five file cards, I don't know. But rehearsed or not, it sounded like a pretty typical case to me. Seems this Link fellow owed a couple of thousand bills to a lady loan shark, name of Fast Eydie. Gambled a lot. Played the ponies mostly. Lost his shirt a lot too, not to mention a few dozen sweaters. Cardigans mostly, she told me. Spent a lot of moolah on dames too. Saw one steady—a hooker name of Olga Nifk, who worked out of a joint on Forty-eighth Street called the Brass Knuckle.

When she'd finished giving me the low-down, she put the file cards back in her pocketbook and looked me right in the eye, the left one to be exact.

"You think you can find him, Mr. Slade?" she asked, her doelike eyes begging me to say yes.

13

"Depends on how much dough you got," I said.

She smiled confidently and pulled four crisp century notes out of her purse and handed them over. "Will that cover it?" she asked.

"Actually, my starting rate is four hundred dollars and ninety-nine cents a day, plus expenses," I said, "but I'll trust you for the ninety-nine cents. By the way, you got a snapshot of the kid on ya?"

She nodded and produced a photo. It must have been taken some time ago, because it showed her brother in a crib playing with a teddy bear. I figured it would come in handy someday for identification, so I took it from her and stuck it in my wallet.

"Call me if I can be of any help at all," she said, getting up and moving toward the door. "My phone number's on the back of the photograph."

As I watched her well-rounded posterior swish hypnotically through the doorway and down the stairs, I knew instinctively I'd be using that phone number sooner or later.

❑

As soon as she'd left, I got up off my own posterior and peered through the Venetian-blind slats down at the street below. Parked right in front of my building was a long black limousine with smoked windows and a uniformed chauffeur who looked like Wilt Chamberlain's big brother standing in front of it. I watched as the Smith dame— if that was really her name—strode out of the building and into the back seat of the limo. As the car pulled away, I wrote down the license number on a piece of paper.

It read "BH."

You don't have to be a genius to know that Mary Smith's initials are not BH. Not even if she was an incredibly bad speller. I've been in this business long enough to know that if you want to stay alive you don't trust anybody, especially people who lie about their names when you first meet them. And there was definitely something fishy about this "Smith" dame.

But I had a job to do, so I didn't worry about it. It was getting close to lunchtime, so I folded the four C notes into a tight wad, stuck them in my underpants and headed down Forty-second Street. It was a warm balmy day, and, as usual, all the scumbags were out on the street—hookers, pimps, junkies, attorneys, the usual low-lifes. I walked fast and did my best to ignore them, but sure enough, when I got to the corner of Forty-third and Seventh Avenue the light changed and a strung-out junkie stumbled over to me while I was waiting for the WALK sign to flash on.

"Hey, bro," he said in a deep whisper that was barely audible, "could ya gimme a little smack?"

I was in a good mood, so I did what he asked—I smacked him. Right in the chops.

By the time I made it to Forty-fourth, my stomach was singing the aria from Beethoven's *1812 Overture,* so I stopped into my favorite greasy spoon and ordered my usual blue-plate special—a pig's knuckle sandwich on rye with a side order of sauerkraut and a Bud. I wolfed the food down like it was my first meal in two weeks, made a little small talk with the waitress, a skinny little bleach-blonde named Denise, and topped it all off with a piece of chocolate layer cake and a cup of coffee. I guess I was hungry, because I felt much better afterward. Like I always say, there's nothing like a little food to make a guy feel nourished.

I was only four blocks away from the Brass Knuckle Bar, so I was there in no time. It was one of those dark, woody joints with lots of whips nailed to the walls for decoration. I figured it was one of those hangouts that cater either to S&M freaks or lion tamers, one or the other. It certainly wasn't my kind of place, but I was on a case, so I casually made my way to the bar, figuring that at least the bartender would be regular.

I was wrong. The bartender had on a black leather vest with spikes sticking out of it and a hat that looked like it had once belonged to the King of the Vikings. I wondered what his mother would say if she saw him.

"Can I help ya, Mac?" he asked none too friendly. I didn't know how the hell he knew my name was Mac, but I let it slide.

"Yeah," I said. "I heard a dame named Olga Nifk hangs out in this joint."

"Could be," he said. He was a coy one all right. A real cutie. "How much is it worth to ya?"

I sighed. Everybody's a salesman these days. I reached into my pocket, took out a dime and slammed it on the counter. For some reason he just looked at it.

"What are you, the Tooth Fairy?" he asked.

I laughed. "The last guy who called me a fairy spent the last two weeks in the hospital," I said, making a fist and bashing it menacingly into the open palm of my other hand.

This time he laughed and hung his dish-rag on one of the spikes sticking out of his vest. "Sounds to me like you're askin' for a knuckle sandwich," he said.

"No thanks," I said. "Just had one."

Don't ask me why, but this really got his goat. He reached over the bar, grabbed my neck with one beefy hand and made a fist with the other.

"Look, pal," I said, choking slightly, "don't force me to read you the Riot Act."

"Go ahead," he said. "Read it."

With my free hand I searched my pockets, but they were empty. "Must have left it in my office," I said. "I could run over real quick and get it."

"Tough luck," he said, about to slam me. I would have decked the sonovabitch right there and then, but before I could decide whether to belt him with my right or my left, I heard a voice from behind me, a female voice. It said, "It's all right, Spike. Let the poor mug go."

I didn't much care for being referred to as "mug," much less as a poor one, but I figured I wasn't in much of an arguing position. Reluctantly, Spike released his grip and lowered his fist. That'll teach him to mess around with the likes of me, I thought to myself as I straightened out my collar and turned around to see whose mouth the voice had come out of. It was a dame all right, sitting by herself in a dark, secluded corner of the joint. I made my way over to her and sat down.

"I'm Olga Nifk," she said. I looked her over. Even if you were blind, you could tell she was a hooker, just from the noxious odor of her cheap perfume. I figured she was about forty, but doing her best to come off like she was only thirty-eight. Peroxide blond, long dangerous-looking fingernails, cheap jewelry, and enough makeup to paint a two-bedroom house and garage—the whole sordid package.

"You lookin' for a good time, Mac?" she said. It was starting to get to me—*everybody* in this joint knew my goddamn name.

"Some other time, sweetheart," I said. "I'm looking for a guy."

"Then you'd be better off across the street at the Gay Blade Tavern."

"That's not what I meant," I said. "I'm a private dick."

"Don't worry," she said, "they'll respect your privacy."

Somehow, I wasn't coming across to her. "You don't understand," I said. "I'm a detective and I'm looking for a missing person."

She didn't say anything. She just drained the last few drops out of her highball. I took it as a hint.

"Can I buy you another round?" I asked.

"Only if you join me," she said. I nodded and she glanced over at Eric the Red at the bar. "Hey, Spike," she crooned. "Another double for me and a . . ."

"Mai Tai," I offered.

". . . Mai Tai for my friend," she said. "And, Spike, lemme know if Michael Finn comes in later, OK?"

Don't ask me why, but I had a feeling I'd heard that name before—Michael Finn. It sounded familiar. I didn't linger on it, though—I had more pressing business at hand.

After the drinks came, I plucked the paper parasol, the orange slice and the maraschino cherry out of mine and took a polite sip or two before getting down to brass tacks.

"Ever see this guy before?" I asked, handing Nifk the snapshot of Link Smith.

"Isn't he a little cutie pie," she said, smiling and goo-gooing at the photo."

"Never mind that," I said. "Have you ever seen him before?"

"Not me," she claimed. "Never saw him before in my life."

"Never saw this guy hanging around here?" I continued.

"Nope."

I didn't believe her, so I pressed on with the interrogation. "Ever met a john named Link?" I asked.

She thought it over. "No," she said. "I met a Fred named Bill once and a Murray named Biff, but never a john named Link."

She was lying, I was sure about it. If you're in this business long enough you develop a sixth sense when people are lying. I looked her right in the eye and was about to give her the third degree, but just then something strange happened. I started feeling woozy like I'd just taken fifty trips on a merry-go-round. Suddenly, the Nifk dame had six eyes and two noses. Then she had four heads and three sets of lips. I shook my head to clear out the cobwebs, but it didn't do any good. The Nifk dame still looked like she'd been painted by Picasso.

I tried to get up, but my legs collapsed under me like Jell-O. All this time, Nifk was laughing hysterically, through all of her six mouths, and the sound of her throaty guffawing reverberated in my skull like somebody was doing a bongo solo in my cerebellum. I stumbled around the bar for a few seconds, trying to grab onto something for support, but it was no good.

The next thing I knew, I was out cold.

When I came to several hours later, I found myself in, of all places, the locker room of the Dallas Cowboys' cheerleaders. I don't know how I got there or what I was doing there and I had to blink my eyes about ten times before I could believe it, but sure enough, there I was, lying in a pile of damp towels, gazing up at twelve of the most gorgeous dames I'd ever seen in my life, all of them in various states of undress.

I was completely awestruck for about five full minutes, so I didn't say anything. I just watched intently as the cheerleader closest to me reached behind her back to snap her bra on. She was chewing gum with a vengeance and all of a sudden she looked down at me and winked. I cleared my throat nervously a few times, got to my feet and sat down on the bench beside her.

"You were great last night, Mac," she said, taking the wad of gum out of her mouth and parking it behind her ear. "Really super."

"Thanks," I said, eying her suspiciously. She was one hell of a knockout, all right, with long legs, wavy auburn hair and a set of charlies that wouldn't quit, not even on Memorial Day.

Before I could ask her what her name was, she turned to me, dressed in only a bra and panties, put her arms around my neck and gave me a smooch that was all tongue.

"Oh, Mac," she moaned, giving me a hickey on the old schnozz. "You're the best!"

"Thanks, baby," I said suavely. "You're not so bad yourself."

"Kiss me, Mac," she begged. "Kiss me till I can't breathe!"

"Sure, baby," I said. Though I didn't know who she was or how I'd gotten there or what had happened "last night," I sure wasn't going to argue with her, not now, anyway. Sure, I was on a case, but all work and no play makes Mac a dull boy. Shoot first and ask questions later is my motto, as far as dames and guns are concerned.

But just as I was preparing for the next round of heavy smooching, licking my lips and putting my arms around this gorgeous dame's willing torso, the room started to go blurry. I tried to focus, but it was no good. Suddenly everything was totally dark, there was no gorgeous dame in my arms and I was kissing something that felt an awful lot like a floor.

That was when I *really* came to. I opened my eyes as wide as they would go, but wherever I was it was pitch-dark. I held my hand in front of my nose, but I couldn't see it. If the locker-room business was a dream, this was a nightmare.

I kissed the floor one more time just to make sure, and got to my feet. I felt like hell on a soda cracker. My head was pounding, my tongue was swollen and my gut felt like somebody had reupholstered it in Naugahyde.

Shaky as I was, though, I had enough of my wits about me to know that priority number one was getting the hell out of that pitch-dark room pronto. The problem was, I couldn't see a goddamn thing. Frantically, I searched my pockets for a book of matches but came up empty, since I'd quit smoking three weeks ago.

Plan B was simple. I took a few short steps forward until I banged into a wall. Once I was sure it was a wall, I groped around for a light switch. Even though I couldn't see a thing, I systematically divided each wall into sectors and covered the area with my searching fingers. Meticulous as I was, though, I couldn't locate a light switch anywhere.

Then I got a bright idea. Maybe there was a ceiling bulb with a cord. Raising my hands over my head, and moving them wildly in a semicircular motion above me like some sort of crazed Indian praying for rain, I took a few measured paces toward the center of the room, hoping that if there was a dangling cord, I'd find it. But I hadn't taken more than five steps when suddenly I tripped over something.

I stopped dead in my tracks. Directly at my shins was an object of some sort, an ottoman maybe, or a chair. I squatted down on my knees and let my fingers do the walking over the thing that had tripped me up.

It wasn't an ottoman, and it definitely wasn't a chair. Chairs and ottomans, I knew from experience, didn't have noses and ears.

❑

At first, I was overcome by shock and recoiled to a safe corner of the darkened room. Hell, I've tripped over plenty of corpses in my day—stumbling over dead bodies comes with the territory—but I was expecting a harmless piece of furniture this time, and I'm not crazy about surprises.

As soon as I'd pulled myself together, I crawled over to the corpse and started feeling it up. I discovered very quickly that it was a *male* corpse, and if there'd been any light in the room I probably would have blushed. Fondling corpses in pitch-dark rooms is another thing that comes with the territory, just in case anyone thinks I was getting any kind of charge out of it, which I wasn't. Detective work is a dirty business, but somebody's got to do it.

Anyhow, since I was already on intimate terms with the stiff, I figured what the hell and started searching the poor dead guy's pants for matches. If I was going to trip over any more surprises, I wanted to at least see what it was. Except for his breast pocket, the poor guy'd been picked clean by whoever it was knocked him off. A brand-new book of matches was the only thing the murderers left. Thank God for little favors.

For a second or two I wasn't sure I wanted to see the rest of the room—if there was another corpse in there I had a feeling I'd lose my lunch—but I took one of the matches out anyway, closed the cover before striking and was about to shed some light on the subject when all of a sudden I heard footsteps that seemed to be coming from outside.

Just what I need, company, I thought to myself, figuring the killers were probably coming back to bump *me* off and tidy up. Quickly, I stuffed the pack of matches in my pocket and frantically pawed the walls until I found what felt like a door. Of course it was locked, so I crouched to one side of it, the hinge side, so that when it opened I'd have a hiding place. Assuming, that is, the door opened *inside* the room.

From my spot by the door, I heard the footsteps get closer and closer. Then, when it sounded like they were right outside, I heard one of the intruders trying to jimmy the lock open, with little apparent success.

"Stand back, boys," I heard one of them say, in a gruff voice, and the next thing I knew I was being flattened by the door, which, incidentally, not only *did* open into the room but had apparently recently been oiled. If I didn't know better, I could've sworn my nose was sticking out the back of my skull from the impact.

The light from the hallway illuminated the doorway and I could see three men, their heaters drawn, slowly enter the premises. To my relief, they were coppers, two beats and a homicide dick I'd had the occasion to meet before named O'Shaughnessy. Nevertheless, I figured I'd be better off for the time being just staying put behind the door, so I didn't make my presence public.

I didn't have to. O'Shaughnessy had gone right for the stiff and was rustling through the guy's pockets, while the two beat coppers looked around the room for clues. Don't ask me why, but one of them decided it would be a bright idea to look behind the door. He must have been a rookie—any experienced copper would've overlooked that one obvious place. Just my luck to pull a rookie.

"Trick or treat!" I said cheerily as the door slammed shut, revealing yours truly behind it. The poor rookie was flabbergasted—I could tell he hadn't expected to find anything behind the door.

O'Shaughnessy turned around and pointed his gat at me. "What are you doing here, Slade?" he asked as if I'd just crashed his wedding.

"I happened to be in the neighborhood and thought I'd drop in."

"You don't expect me to believe that, do you?" O'Shaughnessy said. He was real swift on the uptake, this guy.

"Should I search him, Lieutenant?" the rookie asked.

O'Shaughnessy smiled maliciously, then nodded.

"Hold your horses there, junior," I said as the rookie approached. "You got a warrant?"

The rookie stopped in his tracks and looked over at O'Shaughnessy for help.

"Search the mug anyway," O'Shaughnessy said.

I put up the palm of my hand as a last warning to the rookie, who was eager to get his paws in my pockets. "I'd strongly advise you to back off, junior," I said. "According to the law, the only way you can search me without a warrant is if I give you permission. Which I ain't gonna do."

O'Shaughnessy gestured for the tenderfoot to back off. "We'll just have to get your permission, then, won't we, Slade?" he said.

"Forget it, O'Shaughnessy," I told him. "I wasn't born yesterday."

"There's no law says I can't ask you a few questions," O'Shaughnessy said, turning back to the corpse. "Who's the stiff?"

"Search me," I said.

"You heard the man," O'Shaughnessy said to the rookie. "He just gave you permission."

"Now, wait a minute here," I said, but it was too late. The rookie had his paws all over me and I was giggling like a two-year-old, since I happen to be ticklish as hell. The greenhorn sonovabitch found my heater right away and held it up for his boss to see.

"Hand it over," O'Shaughnessy said. The rookie obeyed. "You got a license for this thing, Slade?"

"Not exactly a *license*," I said. "A learner's permit. I had a little trouble parallel-parking the thing the first time."

O'Shaughnessy glanced at the bullet hole in the stiff's noggin, then cracked open the barrel of my heater and spun the chamber.

"You seem to be missing a slug, Slade," he said malevolently. "And the stiff here seems to have found one."

"Small world, isn't it?" I asked.

31

"Wise guy, huh?" the rookie said, making a fist.

"Maybe I am and maybe I ain't," I said, sticking my chin out to tempt him. "But at least I'm wise enough to know whose fingerprints are all over that heater."

"Oh yeah?" the rookie said. "Whose?"

"Yours, ya dumb punk," I said. "And your equally inept boss's. Don't they teach you morons anything in police school?"

This really ticked the poor dumb rookie off and he went for my throat, but O'Shaughnessy jumped to his feet and peeled the belligerent punk off me.

"Take it easy," he said as the greenhorn stood sulking in the corner. "You'll get a shot at him at the station."

"Who's going to the station?" I asked.

"You are, wise guy," O'Shaughnessy said.

"That's awfully nice of you, Lieutenant," I said. "But I don't take the train into town anymore. You can just drop me off at my office."

At that, O'Shaughnessy grabbed me by the lapels and held my face so close to his our noses were touching. Though it sounds romantic, it wasn't. "You don't catch on too quick, do ya, Slade?" he said. "You happen to be in a helluva lot of trouble, pal. I'm going to throw the book at you!"

That scared me. The last time O'Shaughnessy threw the book at me, it grazed my forehead and caused a slight concussion. That time, it had been *War and Peace,* not a good book to have thrown at you. All I could hope for was that this time he'd throw a lighter book, a novella maybe or a volume of poetry.

"What's the charge?" I asked a bit sheepishly.

"No charge," O'Shaughnessy said. "It's on the house."

❏

O'Shaughnessy let the rookie handcuff me, and the punk sonovabitch made the bracelets just a tad too tight on purpose. I figured I'd settle his hash later, and if there was any time I'd settle his bacon too.

"You realize, Slade," O'Shaughnessy said as we left the room, "that anything you say will be held against you."

"In that case," I said, "I only have one thing to say: Raquel Welch."

"What?"

"You said that anything I said will be held against me, so I said 'Raquel Welch,'" I said. "Get it?"

"Wise guy," O'Shaughnessy muttered, shaking his head wearily.

We waited outside for the coroner to get there. He was this ancient guy named

Pops, who had hair growing out of every one of his orifices except his eye sockets. You could've made braids with what he had coming out of his ears. He was so old he looked worse than the stiff inside.

Once we got to the station, O'Shaughnessy took me right for the interrogation room and sat me down on the hot seat. I took the opportunity to needle him a little.

"You haven't got anything on me, O'Shaughnessy," I said confidently. "So what if my gat was missing a slug and the dead guy's got a hole in his head. So what if you found me at the scene of the crime. You call *that* evidence?"

O'Shaughnessy didn't say anything. He just left the room, though I had a feeling he'd be back soon.

He was a rotten sonovabitch, O'Shaughnessy, and he'd been trying to get my license revoked for years. He actually came close once a few years ago, actually got my license suspended, but I got it back after three weeks at traffic school. It was a bum rap, anyway—all I'd done was make a U-turn in the middle of the Lincoln Tunnel during rush hour. Big deal.

Anyway, I was right, O'Shaughnessy wasn't gone for long. This time he had one of his pals with him, another Mick dick named O'Malley. The minute they walked in, I knew exactly what they were up to—the old good cop, bad cop routine. O'Shaughnessy was going to play the bad cop. If nothing else, it promised to be good theater.

O'Malley started. "Well, well, well," he said in a jovial tone of voice. "If it isn't my old pal Mac Slade! What brings you to this part of town, Mac?"

O'Shaughnessy was standing next to him, gnarling and bashing his fist into his open palm.

"Why don't you ask your pal the Big Bad Wolf," I said.

O'Malley sat down across from me at the table, folded his hands and smiled at me like I was a two-year-old and he had a lollipop. "I understand you've gotten yourself into some hot water, Mac," he said in a singsong voice. "Homicide rap. That's very, very naughty. You wanna tell me why you bumped off the stiff?"

"You *really* want me to?" I asked in a similarly singsong voice.

"Of course I do," O'Malley said. "I'm your *friend*."

Right, I thought, if this jerk's my friend, I'm Carmen Miranda. Meantime,

O'Shaughnessy continued gnarling like a caged leopard with a nasal problem.

"Okay," I said. "I'll tell you why, Lieutenant, if you really want to know."

"Of course I do, Mac," he said pleasantly.

"I had to do it, see?" I said. "The guy insulted you, Lieutentant."

"Insulted *me?*"

"That's right," I continued. "He said some terrible, terrrible things about you, Lieutenant."

"Go on," O'Malley said, his tone a little less pleasant. "What exactly did he say."

"He said he'd slept with Mrs. O'Malley, been sleeping with her for years behind your back. Told me all the gory details. Then he said a lot of negative things about your sexual prowess."

"Like what?" O'Shaughnessy asked dumbly.

But I didn't get a chance to fill him in. O'Malley, his face flushed beet red, had suddenly leaped over the table in a fit of rage and was in the process of strangling me.

"What the hell are you doing!" O'Shaughnessy screamed, still gnarling. "I'm supposed to do that! I'm the bad cop, you're the good cop! We worked it all out before!"

36

Meantime, while O'Shaughnessy was standing there pouting and whining about not getting to do his thing, *I* was choking to death.

"Grf Frrrth!" I said while O'Malley continued choking me.

"Is that a confession?" O'Shaughnessy asked, perking up. I had nothing to lose at that point, so I nodded wildly.

Inspired, O'Shaughnessy grabbed a pencil and a pad and started writing down every bit of gibberish that spewed out of my mouth while O'Malley, foaming with rabid anger, continued to push my Adam's apple down my throat. Needless to say, I kept it brief.

When I was done, O'Shaughnessy, still somewhat crestfallen that O'Malley had upstaged him, peeled his maniac colleague off me.

O'Malley, still breathing hard and trembling with impotent rage, pointed his index finger at me. "You better pray to God we don't meet up in any dark alleys anytime soon, Slade," he warned me.

I spent the next four hours in the slammer.

his wasn't my first time in the hoosegow. I'd done some time back in 1975 on a loitering rap, so I knew my way around a jail cell well enough to know the two cardinal rules of prison life: mind your own business and never bend over without keeping at least one eye on your backside at all times.

I was in what they call a "detention cell," and the crowd was pretty typical—the usual junkies, fairies, transvestites, drunks and a vandal here and there. Nobody too dangerous, but not a lot of potential for stimulating conversation either. Not that I was particularly in the mood for repartee—I was tired, hungry and I needed a stiff drink.

Fortunately, I wasn't there too long. About five-thirty in the morning or thereabouts, O'Shaughnessy came by with a guy in a coat and tie whom I recognized as Assistant D.A. Marty Travers. Travers was one of these Ivy League guys who hated schmucks like O'Shaughnessy. The cell-block guard was with them and he unlocked the cell door.

"All right, Slade," the guard said as he ushered me out. "You can go now."

I stepped gingerly out of the cell. "So long, fellas," I said, waving to the mugs who were still inside. "Keep in touch."

Travers extended his hand to me, and I shook it. "Sorry about the inconvenience, Mr. Slade," he said. "You're free to go now."

"But, Marty," O'Shaughnessy whined, "we got a confession out of him. Plus the evidence."

Travers looked condescendingly at O'Shaughnessy and pulled a piece of paper out of his breast pocket. "You call *this* a confession?" He started reading it aloud: "Bllfffgrffffrrrrth, hmphcrrrrrr oooooh blllllt mmmmmmmmmph grfff, trppppp

39

mmmmmble . . . Either you need to work on your spelling, Lieutenant, or Mr. Slade here needs a refresher course in elementary enunciation." Apparently Travers found his last statement amusing, because he started laughing.

O'Shaughnessy sulked off, cursing to himself and tearing the useless confession to shreds.

"Again, I'd like to apologize for the inconvenience, Mr. Slade," Travers said politely. "You can pick up your belongings at the desk. All the charges against you have been dropped."

"Thanks," I said. But I needed some information from the guy. After all, I was on a case. "I guess it wasn't my slug after all, eh?"

"Actually, it *was* your slug," Travers said. "But the man had already been dead for hours before he was shot with your gun."

"Have you identified the stiff yet?" I asked.

But Travers wasn't going to be much help. "That's for me to know and for you to find out," he said.

"You mean it's none of my beeswax?" I asked, playing his game.

"You got it."

"Aw, come on, Travers," I said. "I'm on a case here. I've spent the last five hours in this goddamn hellhole because one of your dumb homicide dicks doesn't know what he's doing, and God knows how long before that in a dark room with a stiff. Give me a break. You owe me one, pal."

"Sorry," Travers said shaking his patrician head. "I'll give you a bit of advice, though, Slade. Keep your nose clean."

"Don't worry," I said. "I wash my nose every morning. I got the cleanest nose in New York. You could eat off my nose, it's so clean."

"Good fellow," Travers said. "I might take you up on that someday." And then he was gone.

I collected my stuff—wallet, change, wristwatch, rabbit's foot, lottery ticket, racetrack tip sheet. My heater even had five slugs left in it, though I could tell they'd dusted it for fingerprints. There was a pay phone in the precinct lobby, and I made two calls. First I rang up my gal Friday, Tuesday, and asked her to pick me up. Then I called down to the precinct's forensic lab. A guy who identified himself as Quince picked up the line.

"Quince," I said, disguising my voice with a phony Mick accent, "this is Lieutenant O'Shaughnessy. You got an i.d. on that stiff yet?"

"Which stiff?" he said. "We're wall-to-wall stiffs down here. The joint looks like a wax museum exhibit of a Hell's Angels convention."

"Male, Caucasian, about five-eight, black hair, wearing a three-piece blue serge suit, brown shoes. I brought him in about five hours ago."

I heard Quince shuffling through some papers over the phone. "Oh, that one," he said. "I gave you the report on that one an hour ago."

"I lost it," I said, figuring that that would certainly be in character for a dope like O'Shaughnessy. "Refresh my memory."

"We identified him as Hammer, Mike, Jr.," Quince said.

The information took me aback. Mike Hammer, Jr.! Son of the famous hard-boiled dick? Dead? I didn't let on my shock and surprise, though.

"Cause of death?" I asked.

Quince shuffled the papers again for a second. "Very unusual," he said. "He was boiled alive in water for exactly eight minutes, then shot through the head several hours later, after rigmo had already set in."

"You mean he was *hardboiled?*" I asked, totally beside myself.

42

"That's right," Quince said in his matter-of-fact scientist's voice. "Hardboiled is exactly right. If it had been three minutes, he would've been softboiled. You might say Mr. Hammer is a . . . hardboiled hardboiled dick, if you'll pardon the play on words."

I hung up the phone, awed and confused by the information I'd just received. Mike Hammer, Jr., was no friend of mine; in fact, he was competition, one of the best private dicks in the business. And now he was dead. Hardboiled dead, a lousy way to go if ever there was one. Whoever killed him wouldn't be facing just an ordinary murder charge for this one, I knew that. It wouldn't be first-degree murder, or even second- or third-degree murder; it'd have to be 212-degree murder. Fahrenheit (32 degrees Centigrade). I kept going through it all in my mind, picturing the poor mug getting himself hardboiled alive. Suddenly, though, I realized I was hungry as hell. Even though it was breakfast time, I had a feeling I wouldn't be in the mood for eggs.

❏

Tuesday had the car parked in front of the precinct and was puffing on a cigarette, waiting for me.

I got in, took the butt from her and breathed in a long drag. It felt great.

Tuesday was looking at me and shaking her head. "What happened, Mac?" she asked.

"It's a long story," I said. "Start the jalopy and I'll fill you in."

She turned the key. "Home or office?" she asked.

"Home," I said wearily. "I need a nice stiff drink."

"I could use one myself," she said, and made an illegal U-turn right in front of the police station.

I gave her the whole poop while we traveled through crosstown traffic. It was one of those hot, sticky days, the kind New York City is famous for, so I peeled off my jacket and tossed my fedora in the back seat. I had my window opened all the way down, and even though the breeze was chockful of grime and dust, it felt pretty good anyway.

"Sounds to me like you're being framed," Tuesday said after I'd filled her in on all the details.

"Framed, matted and hung in the museum," I added.

"Sounds like your D.A. friend's got something to hide," she said. "Sounds like

44

he was a little too friendly. Not to mention coy. What do you think it means, Mac? You think he's involved somehow?"

"I don't know what to think," I said. "None of it adds up. It doesn't subtract, multiply or divide either."

"Who would want to *hardboil* a private dick?" she asked. "It's sick, if you ask me. The very idea of it makes me sick at my stomach."

"You must've had eggs for breakfast," I said.

"How'd you know that, Mac?" she asked.

"I'm a private eye," I reminded her. "It's my job to know these things."

It was about six in the morning by the time we finally got to my place. I asked the desk clerk for messages, but there was only one—from my mother. Tuesday and I walked up the six flights to my room, and once we got inside she mixed us both a pair of doubles. I downed mine in one swallow. It was just what I needed.

"You look tired, Mac," Tuesday said. "Want me to tuck you in bed?"

"And read me a bedtime story?" I asked.

"If you like."

I glanced over at her. She was, without any doubt, the best-looking dame I'd ever

45

met. Besides the gorgeous kisser and the full pouting lips, she had a pair of gams that started at her hips and went all the way down to the floor. If that wasn't enough to drive a guy crazy, she had a set of charlies that just wouldn't quit, not even on Easter Sunday. I knew she was in love with me—most dames I meet are—and I guess I was in love with her too, but I had a pretty solid rule about intraoffice relationships and I wasn't about to break it. It sure was tempting, though.

She'd been sitting in an armchair, but she must have interpreted my thoughts, because right then she slung those gorgeous gams around and came toward me. I could feel my tired body rouse as she approached and put her hand to my cheek. I couldn't resist taking her in my arms.

"Oh, Mac," she said, breathily, blowing the words into my ear. "Why do we keep playing this game?"

"Because it's more interesting than Parcheesi?" I asked.

"Don't make fun of me, Mac," she said, all serious now. Her breasts were heaving into my chest, causing slight dents in the fabric of my shirt.

"You know we can't get involved, Tuesday," I said. "What would the others in the office say?"

"What others?" she asked. "It's just you and me up there."

"No it's not," I said. "There's Al the doorman, and Ramona the cleaning lady, and—"

"So what?" she said. "I go crazy every time I'm close to you."

"Then don't get close to me," I said.

"You know that's impossible," she told me, pecking at my neck. "I never met a man like you, Mac. I can't resist you. You're like a magnet and I'm like a big pile of iron filings. The minute you walk into the room all those little iron filings are drawn to your negative and positive poles."

"If Mr. Wizard ever retires," I said, "I think you might have yourself a helluva career in science."

"Be serious, Mac," she said. "I can't go on like this. I just can't stand it anymore."

At that she put her hand on the back of my head and tilted my lips down to meet hers. While we kissed passionately for about five minutes I knew I'd been right about her—she *had* had eggs for breakfast.

Hard as it was, I tried to pull away from her, but before I could she had wrapped one of her perfect gams around one of my imperfect gams and I fell backward on the bed with her right on top of me. Once we were in that position, she started going wild.

"Oh Mac," she was moaning, "you're such a *man*. A real man. So virile, so masculine, so manly. I never knew a more manly man than you."

"Thanks," I said, trying to push her loose. "And I never met a more womanly woman than you either, baby, but this could lead to something we both might regret in the morning, so I think you better back off before we get carried away."

The firmness of my voice told her that I meant business, so she got hold of herself and started breathing normally again. Having this effect on members of the opposite sex might seem like a good thing to most guys, but it can be a helluva curse. Sometimes I wished I was just an ordinary guy.

Finally, Tuesday stood up and firmed out the wrinkles in her dress with her flattened palms. "I'm sorry, Mac," she said, those doelike eyes staring at me for forgiveness. "I don't know what came over me."

"Well, we all have our little lapses," I said understandingly. "You have yours and I have mine and we have ours. We're only human, after all."

"I promise I'll behave myself from now on," she vowed. "Cross my heart."

"Good girl," I said, patting her on the head. "Toss me my jacket, willya, baby?"

Tuesday strode over to the closet and grabbed my jacket. Then she held it up while I slipped into it. God, she was a knockout. I must've been nuts not to go along with her before. If she played her cards right, I figured I might even marry her someday.

"Are we going back to the office now, Mac?" she asked.

"You're going to the office," I said. "I'm going to stake out the Brass Knuckle Bar, see what those two low-lifes are up to."

"But you haven't even had breakfast yet," she said. "Why don't you let me cook you a nice batch of—"

"Don't say it," I said, holding up a restraining hand. "Besides, I haven't got time. I'm on a case, and there's plenty of work to be done."

"Anything you want me to do, Mac?" she asked.

"Yeah," I said. "Now that you mention it, there is. I want you to see what you can find out about these two characters, Olga Nifk and Spike. And if you've got any time

49

left, do a trace on my client, Mary Smith. Got it?"

"Okay," she said, disappointed that I was leaving her high and dry. "But keep in touch, all right?"

I took her gorgeous little chin in my hand and gave her a peck on the cheek. Before she could grab me, I was out of there.

❑

I drove down to the Brass Knuckle Bar and parked across the street behind a stalled delivery truck so nobody would see me. It had turned into a scorcher of an afternoon, one of those days when it's so hot your body forgets how to sweat. On the way, I'd picked up a pig's-knuckle sandwich with a side of french fries, a bottle of Bud, and a cup of java. I figured I'd probably be there a long time and I didn't want to starve to death.

I kept my eye on the bar entrance for about four hours. Not much traffic passed through the door, a few hookers here and there and a couple of Hell's Angels types all done up in leather, plus a lion tamer or two.

By about three-o'clock, the place started jumping. All kinds of weirdos and low-lifes in all kinds of bizarre outfits were coming in and going out. I was getting restless, not to mention tired, and started to wonder if this stakeout was really going to pay off.

I was just about to forget the whole damn thing and head for a shower and a nice cool bed when the Viking King and his hooker cohort suddenly appeared on the sidewalk in front of the bar. Finally. I slunk down in my seat and pulled my hat over my eyes because they started walking directly toward me.

I slunk down even farther in my seat when they climbed into the car directly behind mine. I must have parked a little too close to them, because Spike was swearing that the sonovabitch in the car in front of them had boxed him in. Just my luck—I'm sitting in a goddamn stakeout for eight hours and I can't even follow the suspect because I've boxed him in.

"Hey, buddy," Spike yelled out his window at me, "ya wanna move that boat of yours? I can't get outa here."

With my fedora pulled down low over my eyes, I started my car and gave him a little breathing space. With an ear-piercing screech of tires, he was out of there and down the street.

Every private dick has his weakness. Some aren't too swift with a gat, others have problems distinguishing the real clues from the red herrings, still others don't know how to treat dames right. My own personal Achilles heel happens to be tailing suspects. I'll admit I've had some major bungles in this area—hell, nobody's perfect—but, unlike most professional dicks, I did something about it. Two years ago I took an extension course at N.Y.U. called Advanced Tailing and Shadowing 101, and damned if it didn't help me improve.

Now I've got all the basic skills, but my biggest problem, before I enrolled in the course, was what my instructor called "overeagerness." I'd be tailing a suspect and somehow, don't ask me how, but somehow I'd get *ahead* of him. It used to happen to me all the time. I'd be driving along, tailing some mug, and before I knew it he'd be *behind* me. One of the basic rules of tailing and shadowing, according to the required textbook, is to remain in the "behind mode" at all times. It was good advice.

Unfortunately, that wasn't one of my problems when I set out to tail Spike and his lady friend, Nifk. The second I made room for the bastard, he tore out of that parking space like a rocket, just made the light on the corner of Forty-eighth and Broadway, and the last I saw of his filthy white Cadillac it was disappearing around the corner in a cloud of dust. By the time I pulled out of my space and got to the light, which was red, he'd turned down Fiftieth and out of sight.

I floored the gas pedal the second the light changed and followed his trail, but the goddamn white Caddie was nowhere in sight. I figured maybe he'd turned up Sixth, so I got to the corner and looked both ways, but it was no good. The sonova bitch didn't even know he was being tailed and he got away anyhow. So much for Advanced Tailing and Shadowing 101.

Then I got a lucky break. I had just about given up the search and had headed crosstown toward the East River, more out of following the traffic flow than by design, when I spotted the white Caddie heading up the East River Drive toward the suburbs. Without blinking an eye, I floored the gas pedal and screamed after him, cutting off a bus, two garbage trucks and an old lady on a motor scooter in the process.

I'd messed traffic up behind me a little, but so what? I was two or three cars behind the white Caddie, tooling along up the Drive at about fifty miles per hour. It wasn't much of a speed, but I told myself to keep cool and maintain it so as not to jump the gun and zoom out ahead of the bastard.

It was a warm evening, but there was a decent breeze, so I flipped my hat in the back seat and opened the window. Hot air and soot wafted in my kisser, but it was better than sitting in a steam bath. Besides, for all I knew, the slob was taking me to Cape Cod.

About half an hour later, he took the Westchester exit and then turned toward a ritzy burg called Bedford Hills, a rich guy's town with mansions on every corner and people named Muffy and Biff living in them. But that wasn't where the mug was headed, because he kept going straight on, past Waspville, past two or three more Westchester exits, until he finally turned off at Scarsdale, with yours truly tailgating him the whole way.

I kept about thirty feet behind as the white Caddie tooled through the center of town. He was going pretty slow, as if he wasn't sure exactly what his destination was, but at least he was making it easy for me to tail him.

After going around the block once or twice, he took a left, slowed down a little more and parked in front of a synagogue.

Pretty clever, I thought to myself, rendezvousing at a synagogue. The guy definitely had smarts.

I parked about twenty yards down the street, turned off the ignition and waited. After about thirty seconds, the Nifk dame got out first. She must've changed her clothes in the car, because she was wearing a white summer dress now instead of her hooker getup. She'd obviously put on a helluva lot of makeup too and changed her hairstyle, because she didn't look much like the dame I'd spotted the day before at the Brass Knuckle Bar. A few seconds later, Spike emerged, also in a different getup—a black suit and tie, very tasteful actually for a mug of his caliber. Somehow, he'd not only managed to change clothes while driving, but dyed his hair, lost about fifty pounds and shrunk by about six inches. I suddenly realized that I was up against a couple of pretty clever operators.

I slapped on my fedora and follwed them inside, where a Bar Mitzvah reception was going full blast. I'd seen some clever covers before, but this took the prize. Keeping two or three steps behind them, I went through the reception line, shaking hands with the whole family. Some old dame even pinched my cheek and called me Uncle Bernie.

Inside, I tailed them to the buffet table and made like I was preoccupied with a plate of goose liver pâté sculpted into the shape of a Mississippi riverboat. The whole tacky layout reminded me of something an old colleague of mine once said: "The cheaper the cook, the gaudier the pâté." But after a few crackersful of the stuff, I figured it was time to make my move. I sidled over to Spike and, with my hand in my jacket pocket, stuck my heater in his ribs.

"Okay, big shot," I said quietly. "What gives?"

"I beg your pardon," Spike said. He didn't even sound like he had in the bar the day before.

"You heard me, mug," I said. "And don't make like you don't remember me."

"Is this some sort of a prank?" he asked very polite. Boy, he was good, real good. "I know! You're Uncle Bernie, the practical joker from Toledo, right?!"

"Oh, what fun!" the Nifk dame cooed. She was good, too. She looked like a totally different person. A little makeup can go a long, long way.

"Keep your yap shut, Nifk," I said, whispering. "I got a rod pointed at your pal here and the only joke is gonna be if I spill his guts all over the macaroni salad."

Something in their facial expressions changed and I knew they were giving up the ruse.

"Now what I want you two mugs to do is walk nice and quiet like out to your car. Get the picture?"

Spike winked at Nifk and she winked back. They started moving through the room, smiling as they went. I kept real close to both of them so as not to lose them in the crowd, which was now doing the hora in the middle of the dance floor.

"You're not leaving *already*, are you?" some old dame said as we slithered by toward the exit.

"No, no, Gladys," Spike said in his new voice, winking like crazy. "We're just going out to the car for a minute with Uncle Bernie here. We left Harold's gift there." He was one cool customer all right. They both were.

When we got out to their Caddie, I told them to act like nothing was wrong. "Pretty clever disguises," I said, "but you can cut the act now, because I don't fool that easy. I followed your Caddie all the way out here, so I'm not going home till you tell me what gives."

"This isn't a Caddie," Spike said, ever so politely. "It's a Plymouth."

"You gotta get up pretty early in the morning to fool Mac Slade," I said.

"We *did* get up early," Nifk said. "And it *is* a Plymouth."

"Plymouth, my ass," I said, but I glanced down at the side of the car anyway just to make sure. Damned if it *wasn't* a goddamn Plymouth.

"You certainly are some joker, Uncle Bernie!" the Nifk dame said. "Why, this is the most fun we've had since we bumped into Shirley and Marty Baumgarten in Barbados last winter!"

"Shut up and hand over your driver's licenses, both of ya," I said.

They shrugged, but handed the licenses over. Keeping the gat pointed from my jacket pocket, I suddenly realized that the two people I was pointing a gun at were *not* my suspects but a couple by the name of Murray and Leonora Finkelstein. I gave them their licenses back and took my hand off the gun.

"You can go back to the party now," I said.

They looked crestfallen. "That's *it?*" the dame said, somewhat peevishly. "That's the big practical joke? I don't get it, do you, Murray?"

"No," Murray said. "What's the joke?"

"The joke?" I said. "The joke's on me."

❏

Okay, so I made a little boo-boo. It could've happened to anyone. At least I had the brains to realize I was wrong as soon as I did.

Shrugging and shaking their heads, Murray and Leonora headed back into the party, and yours truly scooted back to his car, which, to add insult to injury, was plastered with a parking ticket. A twenty-eight-dollar parking ticket, no less. It was no big deal, but it made me a little depressed. After all, I'd been on this Link Smith case for only about twenty-four hours and so far I'd spent five hours out cold with a stiff, been attacked by a Viking bartender, a rookie cop and a rabid homicide dick, done an evening in the clink, followed a totally innocent Jewish couple to a Bar Mitzvah reception, and, to top it all off, gotten a twenty-eight-dollar parking ticket. And if that wasn't enough, the goose-liver pâté I'd eaten was playing hockey in my digestive tract. This was definitely *not* shaping up to be my smoothest case. Not by a long shot.

Anyhow, I was hot, tired and depressed, so before schlepping all the way back to the city I decided to stop at a local bar and have a few drinks. I found a pleasant-looking little joint on the main drag, went in and ordered a double. It was a dark, quiet little place, empty of customers except for me, and the air-conditioners were going full blast. Cooled off, I downed the double in a shot, ordered a refill, and decided to call Tuesday on the pay phone to see if she'd made any headway tracing "Mary Smith" and my two suspects who were probably in Nova Scotia by now.

"Are you all right, Mac?" were the first words out of her mouth. That was my Tuesday for you—always concerned about my health and welfare. I must've been nuts not to marry a dame like her.

"Yes, I'm fine, sweetheart," I said. "Just fine."

"Where are you, Mac?" she asked.

"It's a long story," I told her. I couldn't tell her I'd followed the wrong couple to a Bar Mitzvah reception in Scarsdale. After all, I was her boss and I had to keep up the image. I felt lousy about it, but that's the way it had to be.

"You didn't follow the wrong car again, did you, Mac?" she asked. Damn, she was a smart cookie!

"Of course not," I said. "That's a thing of the past, baby. That's yesterday's news." I knew she was referring to that time I followed the wrong car from Manhattan to Phoenix, Arizona. Took me four days. When I got there and realized it was the wrong car, I was so ticked off at myself I socked this guy's pickup truck and put my hand out of commission for three weeks.

"Listen, baby," I said, trying to change the subject as quickly as possible. "Did you get any info on the Smith dame or my two leads yet?"

"Couldn't get anything on Nifk and her

61

boyfriend yet, but I'm still working on it," she said. "I got some dirt on the Smith dame, though."

"Spill."

"Well, for starters, you were right, her name isn't really Mary Smith. It's Brigitte Hackensacker of the well-to-do Hackensacker family of Hackensack."

"Interesting," I said. "Go on."

"She lives by herself in Greenwich, Connecticut. Husband died a few years ago. Suicide. Shot himself in the back with a bow and arrow."

"Sounds suspicious," I said, trying to picture a guy shooting himself in the back with a bow and arrow. It wasn't as odd as it sounded—I'd done it myself once by accident.

"That's about it, Mac," she said. "What's your next step?"

"My next step is hanging up the phone," I said. "Then I think I'll pay our Miss Hackensacker a call. See if I can pin her down."

"Shouldn't be too hard," she said, "as long as you keep her shoulders to the mat for the ten count."

"Thanks for the advice," I said. "See you later, baby."

"Be careful, Mac," she said. "And call me if you need anything else."

"You got it, baby."

I hung up, paid my bill and drove off down the main drag until I saw the Thruway signs. Greenwich wasn't too far away from Scarsdale, so I figured I'd be there in about fifteen minutes if traffic wasn't too bad. I had a few pertinent questions to ask *Ms.* Hackensacker, not to mention a few impertinent questions, the most important being why she'd lied to me about something as basic as her name. If there's one thing I can't stand it's lying, especially from a client. Trust is as important in dick work as it is in any other field, maybe even more so.

The street she lived on had to be the ritziest in town. Greenwich is a rich man's haven to begin with, but her neighborhood was Mansion Row. I never saw so many mansions on one street in my life. You had to be a millionaire just to afford a mailbox on that block.

The Hackensacker estate was one of the most ostentatious spreads in the neighborhood. The house itself was separated from the street by a wide manicured lawn that must've gone on for about a mile. A long paved drive wound up to the place and spilled out under a portico supported by four white Greek columns. A thick wrought-iron security gate kept the trespassers and solicitors out.

I pulled up to the gate and was just about to announce myself into the intercom system when I noticed something funny. Parked in front of the estate entrance in the shade of the portico was a car.

It was the white Caddie.

❏

I didn't know what was going on, but I sure as hell wasn't going to make my presence known until I'd had a chance to do a little reconnaissance. So I backed my car up, parked about fifty yards down the street, out of sight of the estate, and took a little stroll around the outer perimeter of the property to find a break in the fence.

Unfortunately, the high iron rails were pretty well maintained and I couldn't locate a soft spot anywhere, so climbing over the sonovabitch was the only solution. It was a bastard of a fence too—each rail had a nice pointy barb at the tip. I knew if I slipped up here I'd be singing soprano in the church choir the rest of my life.

I used a tree stump for support and hoisted myself up and over the rails in a few seconds. Once on the property, I hid behind a hedge and cased the area to make sure the coast was clear. Nobody was around, so I darted from tree to hedge, from hedge to rosebush, and from rosebush to tree until I'd crossed the wide expanse of the garden and found myself near the north wall of the mansion.

My plan was to eavesdrop on the Hackensacker dame and her visitors from outside, assuming there was an open window somewhere. Each side of the great house was lined with thorny rosebushes, so, being careful to keep the thorns out of my face, I crawled under the prickly plants until I was right next to the wall. My next step was to locate the right window.

I got lucky. The very first window I came to was the right one. I crouched low, took off my fedora and watched. Inside, the Hackensacker dame was talking to none other than the two scumbags from the Brass Knuckle, Nifk and her henchman, Spike. They seemed to be arguing about something, but I couldn't hear a word since the window was shut tight. The Hackensacker dame looked scared, but Nifk and her pal were smiling. Finally, Hackensacker went over to a bureau, opened a drawer and took out an envelope which she handed to Nifk. Nifk opened it, glanced inside at the contents, then stuffed it into her cleavage, which was already bulging with several other envelopes, a newspaper and a playbill from the Ice Capades. For a dame like that, a handbag would've been a sound investment.

That was the last thing I saw, because right then I heard a slight hissing sound, followed by a slight spraying sound, followed by a wet feeling at the seat of my pants. At first I thought it had started raining, but I soon realized that that was impossible since the water was coming from the ground. It took me a few split seconds to put it together, but I finally knew what was happening: the gardener had turned on the sprinkler system and I was crouched right in the middle of it with one of the sprinkler heads about three inches from my butt. If you've ever had a fleet enema with your pants on, you'll know exactly what it felt like.

Slapping my fedora back on and wishing like hell I wore a raincoat like most other dicks, I bolted out of there and, keeping well hidden, made my way to the front of the mansion. But I was two seconds too late, because Nifk and her Viking pal were screeching down the long drive toward the main gate by the time I got there.

Sopping wet, I rang the front doorbell, half afraid that I'd get electrocuted in the process. An ancient butler answered the door and gave me a look like I was somebody who'd just been in a shipwreck.

"May I help you, sir?" he asked.

"Is the lady of the house in?" I asked stepping by him and into the parlor. A puddle formed around my feet. I took off my hat, wrung it out and handed it to him.

"Who shall I say is calling, sir?" he asked, taking the fedora delicately between his long index finger and thumb like it was a dirty diaper.

"Tell her ladyship it's Mac Slade," I told him, and he was off.

I strolled around the parlor for a few minutes, looking at various formal portraits of old people who looked like they'd just made in their pants. Then I found a table with some booze bottles on it and made myself a drink. I downed it in a shot, then had another. With two drinks in me I didn't care about the scale model of Lake Superior that was slowly forming around my feet or about the squishing sound my shoes made every time I took a step. I didn't care about anything except getting to the bottom of this case and maybe, in the process, changing into a pair of dry underpants.

But I didn't have a lot of time to think about it, because the Hackensacker dame had come into the parlor and was coming toward me, both her hands outstretched to greet me. I shook both of them.

"Mr. Slade," she said, "what a pleasant surprise!"

"Call me Mac," I told her.

"Okay, Mac," she said.

I looked her over. She was some dish all right. I couldn't believe those big brown eyes could ever lie to anybody. She was wearing a diaphanous gown which, whenever she caught the light from behind, revealed a set of gams that just wouldn't quit, not even on Lent.

"And just what the hell am I supposed to call *you?*" I asked. "Mary Smith? Or maybe you'd prefer Brigitte Hackensacker, since that's your real name?"

She looked guilty as hell and I almost felt sorry for her. I felt like taking her in my arms, but I knew it would be a bad idea, and besides I didn't want to get her outfit damp.

"Are you very, very mad?" she asked, pouting.

"Depends on which psychiatrist you ask," I said.

"I had to do it," she said. "It was stupid, I know, and I assumed you'd find out the truth soon enough, but I couldn't tell you who I really am. Not until I knew I could trust you."

"Look, lady," I said, losing patience, "I haven't got time to play little games. Not even a fast round of Chinese checkers. Now, either you level with me from now on or I take a walk. Get the picture?"

"I'm sorry, Mac," she said. "Really I am. Can you ever forgive me?"

She took a couple of steps closer to me and I could smell the sweet aroma of expensive perfume. By this time I was feeling pretty uncomfortable in my wet clothes—mildew had started to form in my armpits, and my belt buckle had rusted.

"I promise I won't ever lie to you again," she said sincerely. "If you'll just give me another chance. Please, Mac."

She took another step and this time she was in my arms. She looked up at me with those beautiful peepers and before I knew it our lips had come together like two cars in a demolition derby. She pulled my body close to hers and I felt the water that had collected in my pockets spill out onto her dress.

"Oh Mac," she moaned, "you're so strong, so virile, so . . . so . . . incredibly damp."

"I had a little run-in with your sprinkler system," I said.

"It looks like the sprinklers came out ahead," she said, smiling playfully.

"Never mind that," I said firmly. "I've been all wet before. Right now, I've got a few questions I need answered."

"Of course you do," she said. Then she kissed me again and let her tongue glide along the inside of my mouth in a way that drove me crazy. Her breath was hot and heavy and I could feel her body shudder uncontrollably beneath my tight grasp.

"Listen," she said in a deep, husky voice, "why don't you take a nice hot bath, climb into a nice dry bathrobe and let me make you a nice dry martini? Then you can ask me as many questions as you like."

Before I could answer, she'd turned around and started walking toward the stairs, wagging a finger for me to follow. Like a good little puppy dog, I obeyed.

After a nice hot bath, I slipped into the sheer white nightgown that the maid had left hanging in the john for me and found a shaker full of dry martinis in the next room all iced and chilled and ready to go. The nightgown was a little tight in the chest and I wasn't too wild about the slit up the leg, but it beat walking around in my birthday suit.

I'd gotten halfway through my second martini when the Hackensacker dame came slinking in dressed in a new negligee. Her skin was rosy and it looked like she'd taken a bath, too.

"I thought I'd slip into something a little more comfortable," she said, coming over to me and running a hand through my still wet hair. "Do you like it, Mac?"

She spun on her high heels to let me get the full view. It was a pretty revealing little getup, and if I could've gotten somebody to shine a flashlight at her backside I would've gotten a view of her whole package. She was a dish all right, with a set of gams that wouldn't quit, not even on Flag Day.

She was still spinning on her heels, waiting for my response, and I figured if I didn't say something soon she'd get dizzy. She knew damn well she was a knockout, but she wanted to hear it from me. Dames are like that.

"It's swell," I said, catching a fleeting glimpse of her sleek white upper thighs as the negligee swirled in the air around her. A lump had formed in my throat and I knew it wasn't phlegm.

She finally stopped spinning and put her arms around my neck. Those big, pouting lips had my name written all over them.

"Listen, baby," I said, peeling her hands off me, "there's plenty of time for fun and games. First, I got some questions I need answered."

"Can't it wait, Mac?" she asked in a low, husky tone of voice. "I don't know if I can stand this much longer. You're driving me crazy, darling."

"I know," I said modestly. "But business before pleasure is my motto."

She looked into my eyes then and must have concluded that I meant business, because she sighed and settled into an overstuffed armchair.

"All right," she said wearily. "Ask your questions. I'll tell you whatever I can."

I turned a light into her face and started pacing in front of her. I can't help it, I've got to be in the mood to conduct interrogation.

"Let's start at the beginning," I said. "Why did you lie to me about your name and what were those two scumbags doing here this afternoon?"

"Which two scumbags?" she asked.

"What do you mean, which two scumbags?" I said. "How many scumbags do you know?"

She started thinking and counting silently on her fingers. When she got up to six I stopped her.

"Never mind," I said. "I'm referring to the two scumbags you were talking to in this room right before I came in."

"Oh, *those* two scumbags!" she said, after a moment's thought. "Those two scumbags work for a person called the Fat Man."

I sighed loudly and collapsed wearily into the nearest chair. "Not again," I muttered unhappily.

"Is something the matter, Mac?" she asked.

"Yeah," I said. "Something's the matter all right. Why is it every time one of us hardboiled dicks gets a case there's always some mug named the Fat Man behind it? It's enough to drive a dick nuts. Why couldn't it just for once be the Stout Man or the Plump Man? I'd even settle for the Hefty Man or the Man of Considerable Girth. Why can't the criminal element use a little originality for once?" I was really steamed.

"Is he dangerous?" she asked.

"Depends on which Fat Man he is," I said. "Offhand, I'd say he's probably dangerous. They usually are. But that doesn't explain why you lied to me about your name, doll."

"I had to, Mac," she said. "Link's in trouble with the Mob."

"Which Mob is that?" I asked.

"*The* Mob," she said. "You know, the

Mob that eats spaghetti and breaks people's kneecaps. Or is it the other way around?"

"Oh, *that* Mob."

"Anyhow," she continued, "the Fat Man knows where Link is hiding out, and as long as I keep paying up he'll keep his mouth shut."

My mind was working overtime as I struggled to put the pieces of the case together. Suddenly, I came to a brilliant conclusion. "Sounds a little like blackmail to me," I said. "That's against the law, you know."

She looked at me in a funny way, as if she couldn't believe anybody could be that smart, but I didn't let it divert my attention from the one thing that continued to bother me. "I still don't understand why you lied about your name," I said.

"I didn't know I could trust you at first," she said. "What if you were working for *them?* I just had to play it safe, Mac. Can't you see?"

"Sure, I can see all right," I said, "but what does my vision have to do with it?" I wanted to believe her, but I just wasn't sure she was on the level. With those gorgeous, innocent eyes and those great gams she could probably make a guy believe anything.

I had one more question. This one had to do with the stiff I'd spent the night with, but I didn't tell her about that.

"Ever hear the name Hammer?" I asked. "Mike Hammer, Jr.?"

"No," she said abruptly. This time I knew she was lying. She had answered just a little too quickly. "Why do you ask?"

"Just curious," I said. "One more question: Was I the first dick you went to on this case?"

"Yes," she said, and again I had the feeling she wasn't telling the truth. But I let it pass for now. I'd gotten enough out of her for the time being.

She sidled over to me then and put her long-nailed hand up the slit in my nightgown, letting it rub seductively against my exposed thigh. I knew damned well what she wanted, but I had a pretty strict rule about client–dick relationships. Before she could get her motor running full steam, I reached over for my jacket and stuck my hand in the breast pocket.

"Are you giving me the brush, Mac?" she asked petulantly.

"I'm afraid so, baby," I said, pulling a tortoiseshell hairbrush out of my jacket pocket and handing it to her. She looked at it for a moment, then ran it through her long silky hair a few strokes. I watched her for a moment, slipped my pants on and bolted out of there.

❏

The sun was just popping up by the time I got to the Thruway, and there wasn't much traffic, just a few trucks and some early risers. I took it real slow and used the opportunity to do some thinking about the case. So far, nothing added up to much. It was like a jigsaw puzzle with half the pieces missing. What, for instance, did Link Hackensacker have to do with the killing of Hammer? As far as I knew, the Hackensacker kid was hiding out from the Mob because he couldn't pay off his gambling debts and the goons were after him. But how did that tie in with the Fat Man and his gang of hoodlums? And did the Fat Man, whichever Fat Man he was, really know where the Hackensacker kid was hiding out or was he just bluffing? And why didn't the Hackensacker kid make contact with his sister or hide out some-place else? Maybe the kid was dead and the Fat Man was just trying to make some easy dough on the situation. Maybe the Hackensacker dame had gone to Hammer first and Hammer had found out more than he was supposed to, so the Fat Man had knocked him off. And what if *I* found out more than *I* was supposed to? Would they knock me off, too? And if they did, would they hardboil me, poach me or make me sunny side up? Unfortunately, I didn't have an answer for any of those questions, but I've been in this business long enough to know what my next step had to be: I had to get some clues.

By the time I got back to my apartment it was about nine o'clock, and since it was Wednesday I called Tuesday, my gal Friday, to check in with her. Maybe she'd turned something up overnight, some little clue that would make all this confusion a little bit clearer.

"I've been so worried about you, Mac," she said. "Are you okay?"

"Just fine, babe," I said. "I got a few answers out of the Hackensacker dame, but nothing to go on."

"Is she beautiful, Mac?" she asked.

"She's okay," I said, "but I gave her the brush."

"Hair, scrub or lint?"

"Hair," I said. Tuesday breathed a sigh of relief. She was the jealous type.

"Listen, sweetheart," I continued, "I got

a lot of questions and not a single decent answer so far. You got anything helpful to give me on the Nifk dame and her side-kick?"

"A few little tidbits," she said. I grabbed a pencil and a pad off my night table. "Olga Nifk works under several aliases, including Peaches O'Leary, Bubbles Abramowitz and Doodles Dershowitz. She was on the striptease circuit for a few years in the sixties. To make ends meet, she started dealing drugs—the usual stuff, Lomotil, Dram-amine, a few antibiotics. Then she got mixed up with a bad crowd and now she does odd jobs for a guy called the Fat Man."

"What about Spike?" I asked.

"His real name is Olaf Gewurtztraminer, alias Al Fresco, alias Rick Shaw, alias Gene Poole, alias Hugo Furst, alias Pete Moss, alias Shel Gayme, alias Lance Boyle, alias Bud Insky. He's got a master's degree in Scandinavian history from Columbia, class of 'seventy-one. Wrote a book on the Vikings, then spent two years at a funny farm upstate. Diagnosis: schizophrenia—half of him was Ingmar Bergman, the other half was Ingmar Johansson. The Johansson personality eventually prevailed by beating up the

Bergman personality, and he was discharged in 1979. Took up with the Nifk dame and now does odd jobs for the Fat Man, too."

"Interesting," I said. "Got anything else?"

"I checked with the cops," she said. "Both of them have records."

"What kind of records?" I asked.

"Mostly LPs. Jazz, rock, classical, a few easy-listening hits, couple of forty-fives."

"No tapes?"

"No tapes."

"Hmmmm," I said, going over the information in my mind, adding it to the clutter that was already there.

"That's it, Mac," Tuesday said. "What do you want me to do next?"

"See if you can find out anything about the Fat Man. I know there are tons of Fat Men in town, but I really need to know which Fat Man we're talking about. See if you can narrow it down to two or three Fat Men, and I'll take it from there."

"I'll try, Mac," she said. "But it'll be tough."

"Give it your best shot, sweetheart," I said. "That's all I expect."

"What's your next step, Mac?"

"I thought I'd pay a little call on the

Hackensacker kid's bookie, Fast Eydie. I don't think it'll turn up much, but it's all I got to go on."

"Keep in touch, Mac," Tuesday said. "And watch yourself. I don't want you to end up like Hammer."

"Don't worry, baby," I said, laughing. "I'm too hardboiled to be hardboiled."

❏

I knew from my contacts on the street that Fast Eydie worked out of a pool hall in one of the worst sections of the Bronx. I wasn't expecting to get much out of her, because, as far as I could tell, except for the gambling she was clean. No arrests, cardiac or otherwise, and generally the cops didn't bother her much. In fact, I knew a few flatfeet who utilized her services regularly.

Don't ask me why, but I was expecting her to be the usual bleached-out, boozed-out older dame with varicose veins and a gravely voice. Maybe I'd seen too many Bogart movies. But the dame I found sitting at the end of the bar in that pool hall was anything but bleached-out, boozed-out, varicosed or gravel-voiced. In fact, she was a knockout, with a build that wouldn't quit, not even on Passover.

She was the only one at the bar, so I

went right over to her. "Buy you a drink?" I asked, in my suavest, most nonchalant voice.

"Go fly a kite, Mac," she said brusquely. "This ain't a singles bar and I ain't lookin' for somebody to talk astrology with."

I don't know how she knew my name, but I let it pass. "I don't have my kite with me," I said. "I left it in my sandbox with my Erector set."

I could tell she was the kind of dame who appreciated a good round of patter. "You must be a private dick," she said. "Only a private dick would say something that dumb."

"Good guess," I said. "Name's Slade. Mac Slade."

I extended my hand, but she didn't take it. I liked her. She was beautiful, but she was tough.

"Look, Sludge, or whatever your handle is," she said. "I don't like dicks nosing around in my racket, get the picture? I'm clean, see, clean as a whistle. Ain't no law says I gotta sing for you."

"Who's asking you to sing?" I said. "All I want from you is some information."

"Yeah, well, you came to the wrong dame," she said. "I don't know nothin' about nothin', see?"

"Look, baby," I said firmly, "I know you're a tough broad with plenty of street smarts, but you can cut the act. Sure I'm a dick, but I know all about your racket and if you don't spill for me I can arrange it so you'll have to take it on the lam pronto if you don't want to do time up the river. Let's face it—you and me, we speak the same language."

"What language is that?"

"I think they call it street gibberish," I said.

My little speech seemed to bring her around. Though she was doing her best to hide it, a flicker of a smile played across her full kissable lips. "All right, tough guy," she said. "What's on your mind?"

"Tell me what you know about Link Hackensacker," I said.

"What's to tell?" she said. "He's one of my best clients. Betted on everything— horses, dogs, cats, frogs. Lost more than he won. I'd always figured he had a lot of dough of his own, but then I heard he was in trouble with the Mob sharks. They were putting the bite on him and he was running scared. Asked me if I could hide him out for a while, but I told him it wouldn't be ethical, conflict of interest and all that. Last time I saw him, must've been about three weeks ago, he'd come in to tell me he was going away for a while. Laying low until the Mob goons gave up looking for him. That was the last time I heard of him until about ten days ago."

"What happened ten days ago?" I asked.

"This other dick, name of Hammer, comes in and asks me about Link. Then I read in the paper that somebody'd croaked the dick. Are they gonna croak you too?"

I laughed. "What do you think?" I asked.

"You really wanna know?" she asked. I nodded. "If I were you, I'd stay home and keep the doors locked until this thing blows over."

I laughed again and put my hand on top of hers. "I appreciate your concern," I said. "In fact, I appreciate it so much, how's about you and me grabbing some dinner tonight? After that, we could go up to my place for a nightcap and see what develops."

She didn't say anything. She just reached into her handbag and handed me a toothbrush. I took it reluctantly, knowing exactly what it meant.

❏

I wasn't used to getting the brush from dames, but I figured it would come in handy sometime, so I stuffed it in my jacket pocket along with the bristle brush and the lint brush that were already in there, and made my way out of the pool hall. It was late afternoon and the streets were crowded with people going home from work. On the stroll to where I'd parked my heap, I thought about what Eydie had told me. I had to admit, it didn't add up to very much, except for the bit about how Hammer had already grilled her the week before. I'd had a hunch he'd been on this case when he bit the big one, and she'd confirmed it for me. But what did that mean, other than I was probably in some danger myself if I found out too much? But considering how the case was going so far, I had nothing to worry about.

One thing I knew for sure, though—the Hackensacker dame had lied to me again. She *had* hired Hammer before she'd come to me. Only why hadn't she leveled with me after I'd given her the third degree?

I got into my jalopy, made an illegal U-turn and decided to stop into the office for a while before going home. Traffic was ridiculous, so it was slow going until I got to the bridge. The other lane was faster than the one I was in but impossible to get into, so I just tooled along with the rest of the morons at twenty miles an hour and hoped it would thin out by the time I got to mid-town.

When I finally pulled off the bridge, I heard a loud bang that seemed to come from a Chevy in the fast lane. It sounded like the guy had blown a tire, but when I glanced in the rearview to have a look-see, the Chevy sped up and tore by me at a clip.

Two seconds later I noticed that my windshield had a bullet hole in it.

I've been in this stinking business for over fifteen years and I've been shot at plenty of times, so this particular episode didn't rattle me one little bit. Calmly, I continued driving along as if nothing had happened. Calmly, I parked my jalopy outside my office. Calmly, I schlepped up the twelve flights to my floor. Calmly, I entered my office foyer, where Tuesday stood quietly by her desk leafing through a file cabinet. And calmly, I fainted dead away on her desk.

When I came to half an hour later, I found myself being cradled in Tuesday's soft arms, my forehead plastered with a cold, wet cloth.

"What happened?" I asked as my eyes began to focus on my surroundings.

"You fainted," Tuesday said in a quiet voice. "It could have been fatal. You missed falling on my memo spike by less than an inch."

Slowly, it all started to come back to me in bits and pieces. "Somebody took a shot at me in town," I said. "Just after the Triborough Bridge."

"Did you see who it was?"

"No," I admitted. "I didn't even get a decent make on the car. It swung up behind me and I thought it had blown a tire or something."

"Any hunches, Mac?"

"A few," I said. "Let's analyze it logically. Why would somebody want to shoot at me? Simple, to kill me. Why would somebody want to kill me? Simple. To keep me from going about my business. Why would somebody want to keep me from going about my business? Simple. To keep me from finding out too much. And why would somebody want to keep me from finding out too much? Simple. So they could get away with murder."

"Brilliant, Mac," Tuesday said. "But how does all that logic pertain to the case?"

"Beats me," I said disconsolately.

Tuesday removed the cold towel from my forehead and I got to my feet. I felt a little unsteady and supported myself on her desk until I got my sea legs back. Tuesday came up to me and put her arms around my back.

"Oh Mac," she said. "If anything had happened to you . . ."

"Don't worry, baby," I said, interrupting. "Nothing's going to happen to me. Remember, I got nine lives."

"I know, Mac," she said, "but according to my last count you've already used up eighteen of them."

"So that leaves nine," I said, doing some quick arithmetic in my head.

"I hate to even think about it," Tuesday said hesitantly, "but one of these days one of those bullets is going to find its mark. Then what'll happen?"

"Heavy bleeding, I imagine," I said, the image making me feel a little unsteady again. "But don't worry, baby. The bad guys always miss. When was the last time you saw a movie where the bad guys actually *hit* the good guy?"

She had to think about it for a good long minute.

"See, baby," I said, "there's nothing to worry about. As long as I'm the good guy, the bad guys haven't got a chance. Bad guys even miss at point-blank range. They're lousy shots."

"You're right," she conceded. "You're always right, Mac."

That wasn't true, but I let it pass. Meanwhile, Tuesday was still hugging me and I knew from experience that it'd be a matter of moments before she got the hots for me. I figured it'd be best if I cut it off while she was still lukewarm, so gently I pushed her away.

"Listen, baby," I said, "I'd love to stand here all day holding on to your gorgeous body, but we've got a lot of work to do."

"What's on the agenda, Mac?" she asked.

"Two things," I said. "First, I want you to get the Hackensacker dame on the horn and tell her to meet me at Mamma Linguine's in three hours. Next, I want you to put on your best black dress and run over to the Hammer funeral. See if you can dig anything up."

"Nice choice of words, Mac," she said, smiling slightly. "I'll get right on it."

"Good girl," I said. "If you get anything worthwhile, call me at Mamma's."

❑

Mamma Linguine's is one of those dark, quiet joints where Mob flunkies hang out.

Generally, the place is crawling with guys named Vito, Guido and Scarface, the kind of dumb thugs who couldn't win an argument with a house plant, goon types who work for guys named Don Manicotti, Don Canelloni and Don Tortellini. Unlike most restaurants, which have stacks of baby high chairs off near the kitchen, Mamma Linguine's has stacks of crutches for guys who got their kneecaps broke the night before. And, of course, the piano in the corner is missing half its strings. It's a pretty tough joint, and definitely *not* the kind of place you'd take your mother for Mother's Day.

I got there about five minutes early. Luigi, the headwaiter, was leading a big group to a table and yelling, "Gambino! Family of twelve!" but I spotted an unoccupied booth in a dark out-of-the-way corner and grabbed it. I hadn't even ordered my first piña colada yet when this guy I knew, a Mob flunky named Guido Provolone, saunters over to my table fondling a piano wire in his thick, scarred paws.

"Nice to see you again, Guido," I said. "You look like you just had your piano tuned. I didn't even know you played."

Guido wasn't amused. Most Mob flunkies tend to be a little slow in the humor department. He just fondled the garroting wire a little tighter and stared at me.

"If you ever give a recital," I continued, "let me know, willya?"

"Don Corleone wants ta know if you found da Hackensacker kid yet," Guido said.

"How *is* Donald?" I asked. "I haven't seen him in ages. He never calls, he never writes—"

"It's Don," Guido said, "not Donald."

"Don, Donald, what's the difference?" I said. "Maybe you know him well enough to call him Don, but him and me, we're just nodding aquaintances."

"I wouldn't get wise if I was you," Guido said, snapping the wire near my nose. "Don Corleone don't like guys who are wise."

"That probably explains why *you're* still on the payroll, Guido," I said. "I guess the Hackensacker kid owes your boss a lot of dough, huh?"

"Maybe he does and maybe he don't."

"Thanks for narrowing it down to two possibilities," I said. "I appreciate the help."

That confused the dumb hood for about ten seconds, during which time I noticed the Hackensacker dame come in. She was dressed to kill, which, in this joint, was no joke. She had on a tight skirt with a slit up the side, a pair of high spike heels and a blouse that was pulled so tight over her breasts I figured if breasts could breathe these would have to come up for air in a few minutes. There was no doubt about it—the dame had a build that wouldn't quit, not even on Columbus Day.

When she saw me, she hurried over to my booth and sat down. She was out of breath.

"I'm sorry I'm late, Mac," she said. "The traffic was unbelievable."

"Don't worry about it, baby," I said. Guido was still hanging around playing with his piano wire and staring at the Hackensacker dame like he hadn't seen a good-looking broad in five years.

"Miss Hackensacker, allow me to present my close personal friend Guido Provolone," I said. They shook hands. "Guido is an M.D. He specializes in respiratory ailments."

"Pleased to meetya," Guido said, hiding the garrote in his pocket. The dumb lug just stood there like an embarrassed teenager, rocking on his heels, though I could've sworn I saw him wink at her.

"Don't you have a patient to attend to,

Doctor?" I asked him. Dumb as he was, he managed to figure out the clue and disappear back to his buddies across the room. As soon as he was gone, I turned to the Hackensacker dame.

"How've you been, Mac?" she asked. "I've been so worried about you."

"I'm fine, baby," I said. "I got shot at once and almost stabbed by my secretary's memo spike, but other than that I'm okay."

She took my hand in hers and gave it a squeeze. "Oh, Mac," she said, "I'm so frightened."

She had that phony look in her eyes again, so I decided it was time to get down to business.

"Listen, sweetheart," I said, "if you want me to get anywhere on this case, you're going to have to come clean."

"How dare you?" she asked, angered by my words. "How dare you insinuate that I haven't come clean? I wouldn't dream of coming to an appointment without cleaning up first! I showered right before I came into town! If you need proof, I'll give you proof."

At that, she leaned over the table and showed me the area right behind her left ear. It was clean as a whistle. The dame was on the level.

"Okay, baby," I said. "I'll concede you've come clean, but I need some straight answers."

"Shoot," she said.

Instinctively, I ducked. Glancing around the joint, I saw eight guys standing up with their guns drawn, looking for a target.

"Do me a favor," I said. "Don't use that word in this joint again."

"Why?"

"Just don't."

She shrugged. "You were going to ask me something" she said.

"Right," I said. "I was going to ask you about Mike Hammer, Jr. I happen to know that you went to him before you came to me, but I want to hear it from you."

Her expression told me that she knew I wouldn't go for any more lies. "Okay," she said. "I did go to Hammer first. But I have a good reason."

"What?" I asked.

"His ad in the Yellow Pages is bigger than yours," she said. "I swear it."

I knew she was on the level this time, so I just nodded.

"Any more questions?" she asked.

"One more."

"Shoot."

I ducked again, and the same eight morons had gotten up again, their guns drawn.

"Sorry," she said. "Ask."

"Who did you go to after Hammer?"

"You, Mac," she said. "I swear it. I went right to you. You do believe me, don't you?"

I didn't know whether to believe her or not, but I figured if any more dicks turned up stiff I'd know the truth. I could wait.

"There is one more thing I probably should tell you," she said. "I don't know if it applies, but . . ."

"Shoot," I said.

I ducked again, cursing myself this time as the eight trigger-happy goons reached for their gats in unison.

"As I said," she continued, "it probably has no bearing on the case at all, but Link and I are half-brother and -sister. Link's great-uncle is Frank Templeton."

"The police commissioner?" I asked, thunderstruck at the news.

She nodded. The information took me aback. Templeton was not only head cheese of the N.Y.P.D., he was planning to run for mayor in the next election. If he was involved in this mess somehow, I knew I was going to be in over my head. It was bad enough when just the Mob and the Fat

Man were involved; if the cops had a stake in Link's whereabouts, too, it could be too much for an ordinary private dick to handle. It had occurred to me earlier, however, that Detective O'Shaughnessy had been awfully quick to arrive at the scene of Hammer's murder. Could Templeton have tipped him off? A thousand questions entered my mind, but not a single answer exited.

"Does any of this help you at all, Mac?" the Hackensacker dame asked.

"Could be," I said, still trying to make some sense out of it all. She took my hand again and gave it a squeeze. Her lips were no more than two inches from mine and she was looking at me with those plaintive doelike eyes of hers again. Meanwhile, her breasts were still dying of suffocation. I could feel myself slowly melting away.

"There's a hotel right next door to here," she whispered breathily in my ear. But before she could go any further, I plunged my hand into my coat pocket and extracted a lint brush. Reluctantly, she took it and put it in her handbag, knowing what it meant.

I must have been nuts to give a dame like her the brush twice, but I had work to do. Plenty of work.

❏

I was about to walk the Hackensacker dame out when Luigi, the headwaiter, came over to me and said I had a phone call. I gave Hackensacker a goodbye peck on the cheek and followed Luigi to the phone.

It was Tuesday calling from the mortuary.

"Get anything, babe?" I asked her.

"Plenty," she said. "I talked to Hammer's gal Friday. She said Hammer had been on the Link Hackensacker case for days before he was knocked off. She also told me that his last lead had led him to an abandoned beer brewery in Queens. I wrote down the name . . ." There was a pause as Tuesday fumbled through her purse. "Here it is. The Schnitz Brothers Brewery. Elm and Cuyahoga, near Flushing Meadows Park."

I made a mental note of the address. "Good work, sweetheart," I said. "Anything else?"

"Yeah," she said. "Something real peculiar. Frank Templeton, the police commissioner, was at the funeral."

"Nothing unusual about that," I said. "Hammer was the best hardboiled dick in town. Everybody respected him. Even the coppers."

"I guess you're right," Tuesday said. "What's our next step, Mac? Are you going out to the brewery?"

"That can wait till tomorrow," I said. "I think I'll drive uptown and see if I can trace the slug that almost got me this afternoon."

I said goodbye and hung up. I had a lot to think about. The Frank Templeton business scared me to death. Everybody on the street knew Templeton was crooked as they come, but even I had trouble seeing him as a murderer. There was just too much at stake. He was a shoo-in for mayor if he kept his nose clean for the duration of the campaign. Maybe he had a lot to lose if Link Hackensacker sang for the D.A. Maybe he was using the Hackensacker kid to lure the Mob into a trap for some juicy pre-election headlines. But what did any of that have to do with Hammer's death? I could make all kinds of scenarios for Templeton's involvement, but I just couldn't figure what a stiff dick had to do with any of it. Unless Hammer had gotten in over his head, linked Link to Templeton and had to be silenced?

With a million questions rattling around in my brain, I climbed into my jalopy and headed uptown. I figured that if I could find the slug that had almost nailed me earlier that day and then pin down whose roscoe it had come out of, I'd be an inch or two ahead of the game. As it was, I'd been on this cockamamie case for over two days now and I hadn't turned up a goddamn lead worth following up on. Just a lot of unanswered questions.

When I got to where the bridge lets out, I parked my heap and headed for the middle of the street, to the approximate area where I was driving when I heard the shot. Envisioning the path of the bullet as it had slammed through my windshield, I paced toward the sidewalk. Sure enough, there was a bullet hole in the storefont window of a little hole-in-the-wall joint called Lulu's Lingerie Universe.

I entered the store and the first thing I noticed was that I was the only guy there. Just my luck I have to lose a bullet in a brassiere shop. Lucky for me, the sales help were two old bags reading the *National Enquirer* and smoking cigarettes in the corner, not paying any attention to any of the clientele. I could've easily swiped a couple thousand bras and walked right out of there without anybody noticing a damned thing.

The bullet trajectory led me to a huge

bin filled to the brim with discount ladies' underwear. Two hookers were standing there going through some of the stuff, holding bras up to their chests and then shaking their heads indecisively. I figured the circumstances called for bold action on my part, so I strolled on over to the bin and started rifling through the piles and piles of underwear that were heaped there. Naturally, all the dames in the store stopped what they were doing to watch me fumble through six tons of ladies' briefs. Even the two hookers stood there cackling to themselves.

"Takes all kinds," I heard one of them say.

By way of explanation, I held up a bra and made a scissorlike gesture with my fingers where the cross-your-heart strap is located. "I'm in the discount yarmulka business," I said, but I don't think they bought it.

Unfortunately, after I'd torn all the underwear out of the bin, I still hadn't found the damn bullet, so I went back to the storefront window where the bullet had entered the store and retraced the trajectory. Right away, I saw my mistake. I'd traced it too low. It had arced upward from where it entered the store and probably nailed the back wall.

But there was no bullet hole in the back wall. Just two photographs of dames in nightgowns and a mannequin dressed in a black see-through negligee.

That was when I spotted it.

The bullet had ripped through the window, arced over the underwear bin and landed right smack in the mannequin's upper left thigh. After all that distance and all those obstacles, you'd think it would have slowed down a bit, but that didn't seem to be the case. The sonovabitch slug was securely embedded in the dummy's leg.

First I tried to pry the hole open with my fingers, but it didn't work. That sucker was in deep. Next, I took out my car keys and tried to get at it, but that was no good, either. By now, of course, everybody in the shop had once again stopped shopping and was staring at me like I was some kind of pervert trying to get fresh with a dummy. Which, I must admit, is what I must have looked like. To make matters worse, the fact that I suddenly had an audience made me so nervous, I tripped over the dummy's legs and landed on top of her on the floor.

The thing was, I didn't care. The bullet had started to come loose and I was too busy prying it out to notice what was going on around me. A few more seconds went by and suddenly the slug was in my hands. I started to get up when I finally noticed a familiar-looking pair of shoes not very far from my nose. They were copper's shoes.

"Having fun?" I heard a voice say.

I looked up and saw two mean-looking beat cops smashing their billy clubs into their open palms. They didn't look like they were in the mood for jokes, so I didn't make any.

Instead, I swallowed the bullet.

couldn't believe it, but the sons of bitches arrested me, hauled me off to the police station in a paddy wagon filled with hookers, pimps and certified public accountants, and charged me with one count of defacing private property, one count of deflowering private property and one count of disturbing the peace. They even tried to get me on a morals charge, but luckily the proprietor of the lingerie store testified that the dummy was over eighteen years old. Thank God for little favors.

To make a long story short, I spent an

hour or two in the detention cell, paid my bail, pleaded guilty to the charges, and used my one lousy phone call to tell Tuesday to pick me up. While I was waiting around, O'Shaughnessy passed me in the corridor and couldn't resist the temptation to stop and rag me a bit.

"Nice going, Slade," he said, putting his big beefy paw on my shoulder. "Couldn't get a date, so decided to make it with a dummy, huh? You must be pretty hard up, pal. I heard it wasn't even an *attractive* dummy."

"I'm not in the mood, O'Shaughnessy," I said. "It's been a rough day."

That didn't stop the s.o.b. of course. He was on a roll. "There's only one thing I can't figure out," he said, shaking his head.

"Yeah?" I said. "What's that?"

"I can't figure out how they were able to determine which one of you was the dummy."

"Hardee-har-har," I said. "If it'd been you, there wouldn't have been any question."

He snickered to himself, then walked off to go about his business. I was dying to ask him a few questions—in particular how he got to the Hammer murder so fast and who notified him about it—but I knew it would be pointless. Cops like O'Shaughnessy don't usually give dicks like me the time of day.

Just then Tuesday pulled up, and I climbed in her car and practically collapsed in the seat. Before she could even open her mouth I said, "Don't ask," and like a good girl she didn't hit me with a million questions. I managed to catch forty winks while she drove, and it felt pretty good since I hadn't gotten any shut-eye in God knows how long.

She pulled her heap up to the curb outside my apartment and started to get out.

"Not tonight, baby," I said curtly. "I gotta get some serious shut-eye. I haven't had a decent snooze in two days. I'm dog-tired."

"Okay, Mac," she said. "I can take a hint."

If that was a hint I'd hate to see what she called it when I was blunt.

"Did you get anything out of the Hackensacker dame?" she asked.

"A few little tidbits," I said.

"Did she come onto you again, Mac?"

I looked at her. "Don't tell me you're jealous?" I asked.

She blushed. "Just stay away from her," Tuesday said. "I don't trust her and I'd hate to see you get burned."

"Don't worry, baby," I said, "I'm fire-proof. Besides, if I decide to stray from the path of righteousness, you're at the top of my list."

"Promise?"

"Promise," I said.

She smiled. "What's next on the agenda?" she asked.

"First a couple hours of sleep," I said, already yawning at the thought of it. "Then I try to have that slug analyzed by my friend in ballistics. Then I head out to the Schnitz Brothers Beer Factory to see what's brewing."

"Then you found the slug!" she said.

"Yeah, sort of," I told her. "I figured the cops would impound all my belongings when they hauled me in. So I swallowed it."

"Oh Mac, you didn't!"

"I'm afraid so, sweetheart," I said.

"Write yourself a note this time, willya?"

I knew exactly what she was referring to. The last time I'd swallowed a bullet to keep it out of the cops' hands, I'd totally forgotten about it. Next morning I went to the bathroom and, before I realized what I was doing, I flushed the toilet. Fortunately, or unfortunately, depending on how you looked at it, I was staying at an old farmhouse upstate that had a septic tank. Guess how I spent the rest of the afternoon.

"Okay, baby," I said somewhat embarrassed, "I'll write myself a note."

"Don't forget," she said, wagging a finger at me.

"I won't."

I slammed the car door, gave Tuesday a goodbye peck on the cheek and headed for beddy-bye.

❏

I slept like a log—eight gorgeous hours of shut-eye. When I got up, I brewed myself a cup of java, grabbed the paper and headed for the can, remembering that I still had a bullet somewhere in my gastrointestinal system.

I must've sat there for half an hour, because when I got up I'd read the whole paper, even done the crossword and specked out the afternoon race at Aqueduct. The problem was, I couldn't go. I tried like hell, but it didn't help—I was closed for business. Constipated. Of all the times for my bowels to poop out, if you'll excuse the expression. Must've been something I'd eaten.

After a bowl of prunes and a handful of laxatives, the phone rang. It was Tuesday. I could tell by the tone of her voice that it was bad news.

"They found the Hackensacker kid," she said. "Dead as a doorknob."

"I think the term is *doornail*," I said. "Tell me more."

"O'Shaughnessy found him," she continued, anticipating my next question.

"Natch," I said. "Cause of death?"

"He was strangled with a piano wire, locked in a steamer trunk and thrown off the Eighty-first Street pier."

"That would rule out suicide," I said, cleverly piecing together the evidence.

"They want you to get the Hackensacker dame down to the morgue as soon as possible to make a positive identification."

"Swell," I said. "Just where I wanted to spend the morning. At the morgue."

"You want me to break the news to her, Mac?" Tuesday asked.

"No, I'll take care of it, sweetheart," I said. "It's part of the job."

I hung up and lit a cigarette. The prospect of having to tell the Hackensacker dame that her kid brother was dead made me sick. Sure, it was part of this lousy job all right—the worst part. I don't mind getting shot at or beat up or knocked unconscious—all that comes with the territory—but alerting next of kin is a killer.

I stared at the phone for about ten minutes, trying to figure out some way to make the news a little less painful, some way to give the cloud a silver lining. But when you get right down to it, there's no way to paint a happy face on death.

Finally, I dialed the Hackensacker estate. The phone rang about six times before Brigitte Hackensacker picked up the line. She sounded half asleep.

"It's Mac," I said. "Did I wake you up?"

"I'm lying in bed, Mac darling," she said breathily. "Thinking of you."

"I've got some news," I said, my voice firm and at the same time soft. "You'd better sit down."

"But I'm *lying* down, Mac," she said.

"Then get up and sit down," I said. "You're supposed to be *sitting* for news like this."

"But lying is better than sitting," she said. "Lying is one step beyond sitting."

"I know what lying is," I said, "and I know what sitting is and I'm telling you to get up and sit down."

"Okay, Mac," she said. "You're the boss."

There was a pause as she put the phone down and got up to sit down.

"Are you sitting now?" I asked.

"Yes," she said.

There was another pause, but this time it

was my fault. My poor brain was struggling for a gentle way to break the awful news to her. How could I tell a sensitive broad like Brigitte Hackensacker that her brother had been brutally murdered and make it sound cheery?

"Do you believe in reincarnation?" I asked her.

"Yes," she said, "as a matter of fact, I do."

"Good," I said. "Because somewhere on earth, on this very day, at this very moment, there's a baby giraffe being born, or a baby chicken being hatched, or a baby moth escaping from its larva. And one of those little baby animals—the giraffe, the chickie or the moth—is your brother, Link."

There was another pause on her end of the line. "What are you trying to say, Mac?" she asked. "Has Link taken up zoology?"

"Not exactly," I said. "Think about what I said and guess again."

"Oh, I get it!" she exclaimed. "Link's been hiding out at the Museum of Natural History! You've found him!"

"No, no, no," I said, starting to get a little frustrated. "Guess again."

"I'm afraid I'm not very adept at guessing games," she said. No kidding, I thought. "Give me a hint."

I sighed audibly, my frustration mounting. This was going to be harder than I'd bargained for. "Okay," I said patiently. "Can you think of a word that rhymes with 'head' and starts with a 'd'."

"Bed?" she asked.

"I SAID 'DEE' NOT 'BEE,' GODDAMMIT!" I screamed at her. "DEE, AS IN DEAD. DEE AS IN DECEASED! DEE AS IN DEMISE!"

"Well, there's no reason to get testy," she said. "You didn't enunciate properly, Mac. I can't understand you if you don't pronounce your words properly."

I sighed loudly. This was getting me nowhere. It would have to be the direct approach or I'd end up spending the whole day playing twenty questions. "Look," I said as gently as possible. "Here are the bare facts: The cops found Link strangled to death in a steamer trunk early this morning off the Eighty-first Street pier. He's dead. Your brother is dead. Croaked. Knocked off. He's met his Maker, kicked the bucket, given up the ghost, shuffled off this mortal coil, joined the choir invisible. He's cashed in his chips, put out to sea, made his last exit, perished, succumbed and expired. Got it now?"

112

There was another pause on her end of the line, a long one this time. "Mac, are you saying that Link is dead?"

"Excellent guess," I said.

"It can't be true. Oh, Mac, it just can't be true. Tell me it isn't true."

"I'm afraid it is, baby," I said. "I'm sorry. I really am."

"Please tell me it isn't true, Mac," she cried. "Oh, please tell me."

"Pull yourself together, baby," I said, "and take it like a man. Sure it's rough, I know that, but it happens to the best of us. We all gotta go sometime. Look at it this way—your brother's better off where he is now. Nobody can threaten him if he doesn't pay his gambling debts, he doesn't have to hide out from the Mob, and, best of all, he'll never get stuck in rush-hour traffic."

"I never looked at it that way," she said, cheering up a little. "Link hated rush-hour traffic."

"Look, baby," I said, "I hate to ask you this, especially right now in your hour of grief and all, but the cops want you to come down to the morgue to make a positive identification of the body. You feel up to it?"

"I guess so," she said. "You'll be there, Mac?"

"Yeah," I said. "You bet."

I hung up the phone and lit a cigarette. I knew from experience that she was in shock. I also knew that once the shock wore off, she'd probably go to pieces. I wanted to be there to pick them up. Maybe I was falling for the dame. Then again, maybe I wasn't. Only time would tell.

❏

When she arrived at the morgue a couple of hours later, I could tell she'd been crying up a storm. Her eyes were red and the bodice of her dress was damp. She was dressed in black, and even in that dark, mourning color she looked ravishing. I gave her a consoling hug, whispered a few sympathetic words in her ear and led her down to where they kept the stiffs.

We were met by an assistant coroner, Mr. N. Guchi, with buck teeth and somebody's pancreas in his back pocket. "So solly," he said. "Morgue overclowded today. Many many bodies. Last night, big gang war in Blonx. No loom in drawers for all bodies. So solly."

I saw what he meant right away. There were corpses all over the joint. Some of them had been propped up against the walls, others had been seated in chairs. One was standing by the water cooler with a Dixie Cup in his hand. These morgue clerks had a pretty weird sense of humor.

"Name prease," Guchi said.

"Hackensacker," I told him. "Link Hackensacker. O'Shaughnessy brought him in early this morning. Strangulation case."

"Forrow me, prease," the guy said after checking a list on his clipboard.

I looked over at the Hackensacker dame. She had a handkerchief over her mouth, and her skin was so pale you'd think she'd just seen a corpse. I placed an arm around her and we followed the Japanese guy down a long corridor in which several stiffs were standing. They looked so lifelike I almost expected one of them to wave hello. When one of them did I almost had heart failure until I realized it was just another assistant coroner.

Of all the lousy places, they'd stashed the Hackensacker kid in the men's room. He was sitting on the john in one of the stalls. Even though he was dead I couldn't help but think that he was probably having better luck with the toilet than I'd had that morning.

The Hackensacker dame gave him a quick glance, put her hanky to her lips, and folded into my arms. "It's him, Mac," she

115

said. "It's really him. I thought maybe, I hoped that there'd been some mistake, but it's really him. Please, Mac, take me home. Take me away from this horrible place. I don't think I can stand it anymore."

"Sure, baby," I said.

I led her back upstairs and out to my jalopy. I figured we'd stop off at my office for a nice stiff belt of Scotch first. She needed a little pick-me-up and I didn't want her driving out to Connecticut alone while she was in this condition.

Tuesday was manning the phones as we walked by her and into my office. I poured a couple of shot glasses and handed one to the Hackensacker dame. "Drink it, baby," I said. "It'll do you good."

She swallowed it in a shot and I poured her another one before she had a chance to put the glass down. She looked up at me, her doelike eyes streaming with tears.

"Hold me, Mac," she said. "I need to feel your powerful arms around me. I need to feel secure and protected. I need your strength."

I did like she said, holding her tight as her tears stained my lapels.

"He was all I had, Mac," she said. "Now I have nothing. No one."

"You've got me, babe," I said. "And I've got you and we've got each other."

"Oh Mac, is it true?" she asked looking up at me. "Do you love me just a little bit?"

I was suddenly conscious of the fact that my office door was still open and that Tuesday could hear everything we were saying from her desk. If there was anything I didn't need right now it was a jealous gal Friday, and Tuesday could get pretty jealous. So I reached up with my foot and pushed the door shut.

"Do you, Mac?" the Hackensacker dame insisted.

I was about to answer her in the affirmative and shower her with fervent kisses, when I got the first cramp. Right in the pit of my belly. It felt like my gut was a locked door and ten guys were trying to get in with a battering ram. Frantic, I peeled the Hackensacker dame's arms off me and bolted for the john.

I must've taken too many laxatives, because what came out made Old Faithful look like a leaky faucet. As soon as I was done, I got up, flushed the toilet and rejoined the Hackensacker dame in my office.

She was standing by the window, and when she saw me she turned those doelike eyes toward me again.

"You haven't answered my question yet, Mac," she said. "Do you love me?"

"Oh my God!" I shouted. "Oh Jesus M. Christ!"

"What's the matter?" she asked, horrified by my outburst. "What is it?"

"I flushed the toilet!" I said. "I can't believe it! I flushed the goddamn toilet!"

"Yes, I heard it," she said. "If congratulations are in order—"

"You don't understand," I said. "I FLUSHED THE TOILET!"

"I'll alert the news media," she said sarcastically.

I was too angry at myself to get into an explanation, so I just settled into a chair and put my head in my hands. I'd lost it—my one and only decent piece of evidence was presently floating around somewhere with the alligators in the New York sewer system.

The Hackensacker dame was steaming mad. She headed for the door.

"You can be a real rat sometimes, Mac," she said. "Here I was pouring my heart out to you, telling you that I loved you, asking you if you loved me and all you can say is you flushed the toilet. You may be a good dick, but you suck eggs in the romance department. Goodbye."

And on that note she stormed out of the office. The funny thing about it was, I think I was falling in love with the crazy dame.

I hung around the office for another ten minutes or so trying to think of a way of retrieving the lost slug without having to get waist-deep in sewage. After all, I'd gone through a hell of a lot of aggravation just trying to get ahold of the goddamn thing in the first place—I'd wrestled with a mannequin, gotten arrested, done four charming hours in the joint, spent fifty simoleons on bail and now all I had to show for it was an acute case of Montezuma's Revenge and a pissed-off client.

Maybe there wasn't anything I could do to retrieve the bullet—that was history—

but I could certainly alleviate the runs and placate the pissed-off client. So, without further ado, I reached into my drawer and took out three things—a pen, a piece of my own personal stationery and a king-size bottle of Kaopectate. Swigging from the bottle of white chalky liquid, I dashed off an apology to the Hackensacker dame, explaining in detail exactly why I had been so excited about having flushed the toilet and apologizing for having destroyed the romantic mood. I signed it "Affectionately yours," drew a happy face on it, and stuffed it into an envelope.

It was still early in the afternoon, so I figured I'd have plenty of time to head out to the Schnitz Brewery in Queens. Grabbing the letter, the bottle of Kaopectate and an empty thermos (just in case there was some drinkable beer lying around), I told Tuesday I'd be gone for the duration of the afternoon and headed out to my jalopy. As I walked by her, Tuesday gave me one of her best dirty looks, but I didn't have the time or the inclination to give her the explanation I knew she was waiting for, so I just kept walking. If she was jealous, I figured she'd have plenty of time to get over it.

Traffic was light, so I tooled up Sixth Avenue, made a right on Fifty-seventh Street and headed for the Queensboro Bridge. On the way, something strange happened. I was stopped for a light on Forty-fifth Street when a poster, hung on a construction-site wall, caught my attention. I didn't know exactly why it caught my attention, but it did. It showed a Broadway showgirl dressed in a gaudy costume, kicking up her legs in a dance number. It was an ad for some kind of Broadway musical, and I just sat there at the light and stared at it for about twenty seconds like I was hypnotized, until the guy behind me started leaning on his horn to let me know the light had changed. I moved on slowly, but the image on that poster stuck in my mind, don't ask me why.

I got to the brewery half an hour later and parked about two hundred yards from the premises. The place looked pretty deserted to me, but I wasn't taking any chances. The whole area reeked of stale beer, so I left the thermos in the car and started to snoop around.

It wasn't too long before I found something. The entry to the brewery was unlocked, so I walked right in, as quietly as possible, making sure to keep in the shadows. Down on my hands and knees, I crept from beer vat to beer vat, slowly but steadily making my way toward a room in the back of the joint. I'd seen the room when I came in—there was a light on and three people were standing inside making what appeared to be some kind of transaction. Two of them I could see clearly enough, my old pals Olga Nifk and her Viking cohort Spike, but I couldn't get a good enough view of the third person to make him out. I knew instinctively that if I could get an eyeful of the third party I'd have something concrete to work with.

I took out my roscoe and crawled closer. There was a boiler of some kind just off the lighted office and I figured if I could make it that close I'd get my view. But I had to be real careful—it was darker than hell in the brewery and if I tripped over something it'd be all over.

Inch by inch I plodded along on my knees, roscoe at the ready, until I got to the vat closest to the lit office. I was within two lousy yards of my destination. To get to the boiler, I'd have to crawl within full view of the three mugs in the office, but when I looked up I saw that they were involved in a fierce argument of some kind, so I figured now was the time. Crouched as low as I could go, I snuck by them and edged my body behind the boiler.

That was when it happened. The boiler was hotter than hell, and the minute I touched it my finger automatically pulled the trigger, my gun went off, and two hundred gallons of stale beer started pouring all over my face from the main vat right above me. The foamy brew completely blinded me and I was unable to focus on my mark in the office. My eyes stung like crazy, and no matter how hard I wiped them I just couldn't see a damn thing. I heard noises, though, coming from behind me, plenty of noises.

The next thing I knew, I was out cold.

❑

When I came to several hours later, I was—you guessed it—back in the locker room of the Dallas Cowboys' cheerleaders, picking up where I'd left off a couple of days before. The same gorgeous doll was groping me, kissing me and whispering come-ons into my ear. While our lips were stuck together with the epoxy glue of lust, she was struggling to undo my belt buckle.

"Oh Mac," she was moaning. "Oh Mac, you turn me into an *animal* . . ."

"Just as long as you've had your rabies shot," I muttered.

"Take me, Mac," she groaned, surrendering her body to mine. "Take me. I'm yours."

I shook my head. "It's no good, baby," I said. "I'm not going to let myself get all heated up only to wake up in the middle of the good part. Contrary to public opinion, I'm not as dumb as I look."

"Don't you find me . . . attractive?" she asked, pouting ever so sweetly and letting her tongue glide seductively over her front teeth.

"Oh sure," I said. "I think you're a knockout, but, you see, baby, this isn't real."

She lowered her hand, the one that was struggling with my belt buckle. "It feels real to me," she said.

"Sure, and it feels real to me too," I continued. "It feels real real. Really. But the fact of the matter is, I'm dreaming this. This is nothing more than a figment of my imagination, you see. I was snooping around in an abandoned beer brewery, somebody smacked me on the noggin with the usual blunt object, and now I'm out cold. Get the picture?"

"Oh Mac, you're being silly," she said gleefully.

I put up a restraining hand. "I'm not the silly type," I said. "This is just a dream. Trust me."

She scrunched up her gorgeous face for a

second, a clear indication that she was thinking. "Well," she said, "if you're right and this is a dream, then if I pinch you, you should wake up, right?"

Made sense to me. "That's right," I said.

"Then I'll pinch you," she said happily. "And if you don't wake up, we can keep on doing what we're doing, okay?"

"Okay."

With that, she moved her belt-unbuckling hand around to my posterior and, using those killer nails of hers, gave me a pinch that was so hard it must've drawn blood. I stifled a scream—I didn't want her to think I was a sissy, not even if she *was* just a figment of my imagination—and waited for everything to start getting blurry on me. But nothing happened. I was still there in the locker room, standing in front of a half-dressed cheerleader with fire in her eyes and a hand on my buns.

"See?" she said, proud of herself. "I told you it wasn't a silly old dream."

I couldn't believe it. I blinked about ten times, expecting her to disappear, but she didn't. I slapped myself on the cheeks twice, expecting the room to go blurry, but it didn't. I even punched myself in the stomach, deliberately banged both my shins against the locker room bench and slammed my head against the wall. Nothing. Finally, I shrugged, said the hell with it, and started trying to get her bra undone. I had it off in a snap, her breasts came tumbling out and the next thing I knew we were both groping for each other on the floor in a pile of damp towels. Her screams of delight were getting heavier and louder, about to reach a crescendo, when all of a sudden . . .

I really came to. At first I didn't believe it, but within moments, once the initial blur of disorientation had faded away like a thin morning mist, I knew reality had once again socked me in the kisser at the least appropriate moment. Whatever cosmic entity controlled my dream life certainly had a hell of a sense of humor, because not only had my love-starved cheerleader vanished, but I found myself sitting neck deep in a vat of stale, reeking beer five feet away from a stiff with a hole in his head.

My first impulse was to get the hell out of the vat before the rancid alcohol pickled my skin. I was drenched through and it was slippery as hell, but somehow I managed to climb out without breaking my neck. The place was quiet except for the pitter-patter of the beer droplets as they rolled off my jacket and onto the floor. Cursorily casing the joint, I knew instinctively that whoever had knocked me over the head had long since vacated the premises.

I didn't stick around to search the stiff, because I figured the cops would be there soon enough and I wasn't in the mood for any wisecracks from O'Shaughnessy. Nor did I feel like spending another night in the slammer. Twice in twenty-four hours was plenty. So I just beat a path for the exit and headed for my jalopy.

That was when I got the second surprise of the afternoon. My jalopy was gone. Disappeared as thoroughly as my oversexed cheerleader. There I was in the middle of some remote neighborhood of Queens sopping wet with old beer, the sun beating down on my head relentlessly, and I'd have to take the stinking bus back to Manhattan in the middle of rush hour.

Thoroughly disgruntled, I started walking until I found a bus stop. Of course it was mobbed with commuters, all of whom took about ten discreet steps to their right when they caught the first good whiff of my scent. By this time, the sun had helped my odor along enough that I smelled like the alley of a fish market during a garbage strike. To make matters even worse, the bus was half an hour late and I had to stand there like a total moron, fending off two stray dogs who thought I was some kind of canine sex symbol.

When the bus finally did pull up, the situation got desperate. Since it was rush hour, the bus was packed full of people, most of whom deboarded the minute I entered the premises. I never saw so many people hurtle themselves off a bus gasping for air in my life. The driver looked at me for a minute, sprayed the area with a can of air deodorizer and finally drove on. Needless to say, I didn't have any trouble at all finding a seat.

It was early evening by the time I'd walked the fifteen blocks from where the bus dropped me off to my apartment. I was exhausted and the dried beer had starched my clothes. With what energy I had left, I walked the six flights up to my place, unlatched the door and headed straight for the shower without even turning on the lights.

I hadn't gotten very far when I heard what sounded an awful lot like somebody clearing their throat.

"Who's there?" I asked, switching on a lamp.

It was O'Shaughnessy, sitting placidly in my favorite armchair, leafing through a magazine.

"You stink," he said.

"Flattery will get you nowhere," I retorted. I peeled off my stiff jacket and unsnapped my suspenders. O'Shaughnessy picked the jacket up, held it to his nose and started sniffing it like it was fine wine.

"It's gabardine," I said, "and the usual method of testing the fabric is by feeling it between your thumb and index finger, not smelling it."

"You'll never guess who we found at the Schnitz Beer Brewery late this afternoon." he said.

"Amelia Earhart," I guessed.

"Philip Marlowe, Jr.," O'Shaughnessy said. "Boiled to death just like Hammer and with one of your slugs in his head."

"Must be contagious," I said facetiously, but my mind was racing. Another hardboiled hardboiled dick. Marlowe, son of the famous shamus Philip Marlowe of Los Angeles, was one of the best dicks in the business. I ought to know—I'd lost plenty of business to the likes of him.

"We also found your car about two miles from the brewery," O'Shaughnessy continued. "I suppose you were having some body work done out in Queens, right?"

"Right," I said.

O'Shaughnessy got up, his playful mood over. "Stop playing dumb, Slade," he said, "even though the role comes naturally for you."

"All right," I said, "I'll come clean with you, Detective, mainly because I'm just too tired to make up a convincing song and dance. I was out there, snooping around. Somebody belted me on the noggin with the usual blunt object and the next thing I knew I was out cold in a stale vat of beer with a stiff."

O'Shaughnessy pointed a finger at me. "If I were you, Slade," he said, "I'd keep my nose clean. Stay out of trouble or we'll have your license so fast you won't know what hit you. You're up to your neck in hot water, pal."

"Warm beer would be closer to the truth," I said. "Hot water is what I'm trying to avoid. Don't forget, I'm a hardboiled dick myself and who's to say the killer, whoever he is, isn't going to boil me next?"

O'Shaughnessy started laughing hysterically. "You?" he said, amused. "Don't flatter yourself, Slade. You're not in the same league with the likes of Hammer and Marlowe. Not even close."

I ignored the slur. I have to admit, though, my feelings were a little hurt, not from what O'Shaughnessy had said—he was just a dumb flatfoot—but by the fact that two of the best hardboiled dicks in New York had been murdered and the killer seemed to be ignoring me. Dumb as it may sound, I felt slighted. I mean, I was a hardboiled dick, too, I'd paid my dues, I'd been knocked cold, shot at, beaten up, the whole ball of wax. Hell, I'd done everything Hammer and Marlowe had done and more. So why wasn't *I* being hardboiled alive? What was I, chopped liver?

"You're chopped liver," O'Shaughnessy continued. "If somebody tries to hardboil you, I'll eat my hat. You're safe, pal. Safe as hell."

I wanted to sock the sonovabitch in the jaw, but being arraigned on a charge of assaulting a police officer was not my idea of how to spend an interesting evening, so I let it pass. I figured I'd change the subject.

"You know something, O'Shaughnessy?" I said. "It's kind of funny how you and your boys seem to get to the scene of these crimes so fast. A fella might even be led to believe you know a little too much."

"Don't be a sap, Slade," he said. "We were alerted by an anonymous caller both times."

I smirked. I didn't believe the bastard any farther than I could throw him.

"Sure," I said, "and the next thing you're

going to tell me is that Frank Templeton doesn't know anything about it, either."

I was fishing for clues, but O'Shaughnessy suddenly looked as if he'd seen the ghost of his dear departed mother-in-law. So Templeton *did* figure in somehow.

"Look, Slade," O'Shaughnessy said, "You're not going to get anything out of me. The only reason I'm here in the first place is to take you in to see the D.A. He wants to have a little chat."

"About what?"

"That's between you and the D.A.," he said. "I told him you didn't know your ass from a hole in the ground, but he wants to see you anyway."

"Thanks for the nice buildup," I said. "What if I don't feel like talking to the D.A.?"

"Then I'll just have to take you in on suspicion of homicide," O'Shaughnessy said, a self-satisfied smirk lighting up his ugly features. "After all, we've got two of your slugs, one from Hammer and one from Marlowe, and your gat is missing two, right?"

Just for the hell of it, I cracked open my roscoe and looked in the chamber. Much to my surprise, there were *three* slugs missing, not two. For the life of me, I couldn't figure where the third one had gone, but I didn't let on to O'Shaughnessy.

"Right," I said.

❑

The D.A. was one of those tall, gaunt Waspy guys, polite on the surface but a real sonovabitch underneath it all. I'd tangled with the bastard a couple of times before, and he was dying to get my license revoked. I knew damn well what he wanted out of me, information, but he wasn't going to get a single goddamn clue, mainly because I didn't *have* a single goddamn clue. The fact was, the dumb bastard probably knew more than I did.

"How nice to see you again, Mr. Slade," he said, smiling insincerely. "Please sit down. May I offer you a drink?"

"Cut the patter, Counselor," I said. "I'm a busy man."

"So I hear," he said condescendingly. "Detective O'Shaughnessy thinks you've been a little too busy for your own good."

"Well, maybe if Detective O'Shaughnessy was a little busier himself, you'd have solved this case already."

O'Shaughnessy tightened his fists and shot me a dirty look. I smiled back at him.

"Now, now, Mr. Slade," the D.A. said calmly. "Let's try to maintain an atmosphere of cooperation here. After all, we're all working on the same case. We're all trying to catch this vicious murderer and put him behind bars so that the streets can be safe from crime and violence."

"Save the oratory for the campaign," I said.

He was unruffled. "All I'm trying to say is that we'll scratch your back if you'll scratch ours."

"My back doesn't itch," I said.

"Well, mine does," the D.A. said. Sighing, I got up, ambled over to where he was sitting and started rubbing his shoulder blades. I'd been through this routine a hundred times before and I was convinced the guy had psoriasis.

"A little lower," the D.A. said. "That's right. Ahhhhh. That feels good. Thank you."

I went back to my seat and the D.A. resumed the discussion. "Getting back to the case," he said. "I presume you've got a few suspects under surveillance?"

I didn't have a thing, but I sure as hell wasn't going to let him know it. "A few," I said.

"Then you've located Sam Spade, Jr.?" he asked.

Hell, I didn't even know there *was* a

134

Sam Spade, Jr., let alone how he figured in the case, but I tried as hard as I could to conceal my surprise. "Maybe I have and maybe I haven't," I said cagily.

O'Shaughnessy stood up. "He doesn't know a damn thing, sir!" he shouted at the D.A.

"Sit down, O'Shaughnessy," the D.A. said. Then he turned back to me, his voice firm and threatening. "Look here, Slade, I want to play ball with you, but you don't seem to want to play ball with me."

"Nothing personal," I said. "I'm just not into sports."

"I'm warning you, Slade," he said, his meanness coming to the surface finally. "Make one wrong move, one moving violation, one lousy little misdemeanor, and you're out of business for life. You're finished! You've mucked up enough of my cases. I'll have your license and your permit so fast you won't know what hit you."

I stood up and put on my fedora. "I don't have to sit here and take this lying down," I said. "If you've got a warrant, then use it. If you don't, I'm out of here."

They looked at each other with impotent rage. They didn't have a warrant, that much was obvious. I saluted both of them in a cavalier sort of way and left them sitting there with egg on their faces.

I hopped a cab home, thinking on the way of Sam Spade, Jr., and how he figured in the case. Frankly, I was at a complete loss, no closer to solving this case than I'd been thirty-six hours ago. Was Spade, Jr., the next hardboiled dick on the murderer's agenda or was he the murderer himself? Instinctively, I knew that the answer to that one crucial question would help solve this case.

When I got back to my place, I peeled my stiff, smelly clothes off and headed right for the shower. That was when I noticed it: two bloody fingernail tracks on my backside, clear as can be. On the exact spot where my oversexed cheerleader had pinched me.

I woke up the next morning confused as hell. The more I thought about this goddamn case, the more tangled up it got. There were a million questions rattling around in my brain and not a single lousy answer. What did the Hammer and Marlowe murders have to do with the death of Link Hackensacker? How did Sam Spade, Jr., fit in? Was Frank Templeton's relationship to the Hackensackers an integral part of the case or just a coincidence? How deeply was the Mob involved and what was the Fat Man's connection to the hard-boiled dicks' murders?

I only knew two things for sure: First, I knew that the Hackensacker dame had lied again, that she'd really gone to Marlowe before knocking on my door. And, second, I knew that I wasn't any closer to solving this case now than I'd been three days ago. If things continued like this, I'd probably end up having to give the Hackensacker dame a refund.

The funny thing was, every time I tried to put the pieces of the case together, I kept coming back to a connection that didn't make any logical sense at all. Somehow, don't ask me how, I had a hunch that Sam Spade, Jr., and that Broadway poster I'd spotted were linked. Somewhere, in the inner recesses of my mind, there lurked a connection between those two things, but try as I might, I couldn't put it together.

Frustrated, I downed the last drops of java from my coffee cup, bit off a hunk of raspberry Danish that had been sitting in my refrigerator since the Eisenhower Administration, and drove to my office. I figured maybe a change of atmosphere would help put the clues together. It was only eight in the morning, but it was already a scorcher, and by the time I got up the twelve flights of stairs I was soaked through with perspiration.

Tuesday shot me one of her standard dirty looks. "What's eating you?" I asked, knowing she was probably still sore about my little tête-à-tête with the Hackensacker dame the day before.

"Oh Mac," she cried, "don't you know? I couldn't sleep all night."

"I hear warm milk usually does the trick," I suggested. I could be a real hard-ass sometimes.

"It's not insomnia," she said. Then she lowered her head shyly. "It's jealousy, Mac. That Hackensacker woman is getting to you, isn't she?"

I shrugged. "What if she is?" I said. "I never promised you a rose garden."

"Yes you did," Tuesday said. "Don't you remember? Two years ago?"

She was right. Two years ago I *had* promised her a rose garden. I said she could have azaleas and hibiscus too if she wanted them. I should've kept my mouth shut. Never promise a dame anything, least of all a garden.

"You're not planning to . . . do anything foolish, are you, Mac?" she asked with a tremor in her voice.

"Like what?" I asked.

"Like make an honest woman out of her?"

"Are you kidding?" I asked. "That would require a gene transplant and about twenty years of electric-shock treatments."

"That's not what I meant," Tuesday said. "I meant, are you planning to . . . marry the dame?"

I sure as hell wasn't, but I was in a feisty mood, so I just shrugged. "She's got a lot of dough," I said.

"Dough isn't everything," Tuesday said.

I'd heard that line plenty of times before, usually from people who didn't have a cent to their names.

"Maybe you're right," I said, "but it sure beats spending the rest of my life chasing scum and low-lifes all over town."

"But, Mac," she replied, "you won't have to scrounge anymore. Now that Hammer and Marlowe are gone, you're the top dick! You're at the head of the class! No more competition!"

I hadn't thought of that, but she was dead right. I was just about to tell her so, but I didn't get the chance because right then there was a knock on the door and a delivery man came in carrying a bouquet of daffodils. I figured they were for Tuesday.

I was wrong. They were for me. From the Hackensacker dame. The card read

"Dearest Mac, Can you ever forgive me for being so silly? Forever yours, Brigitte. P.S. I'm sorry you flushed the toilet."

Tuesday was reading the card over my shoulder and she scowled angrily. To placate her, I tossed it in the trash basket.

"Can you beat that?" I said. "The dame sends me flowers. What the hell am I supposed to do with a bunch of goddamn flowers? A tie, a watch, a pair of socks I could use, but flowers? What the hell does she think I am, some kind of sissy or something?"

"I wouldn't send you flowers, Mac," Tuesday said. "I'd send you something masculine and useful like a power drill or a case of Bud or a pound of chewing tobacco."

Then I got an idea. I didn't want my gal Friday ticked off at me all day, so I extended the bouquet to her. "Take 'em," I said. "Consider it a peace offering."

Like a typical dame, Tuesday smiled brightly. "For me?" she exclaimed. "Oh, how thoughtful of you, Mac! They're beautiful!" She pulled a vase out of her desk and plunked the stinking flowers in it. Dames are all the same, no matter who they are. Pay them a compliment and give them a bunch of flowers and they're yours for the asking.

With that over with, I retreated into my office, shut the door, poured myself a shot of rye, lit a cigarette and started thinking about the case again. Frankly, the whole thing was a mystery to me. A very deep, dark, confusing mystery with all the standard red herrings and misleading clues. Sighing, I stared out the window at the Camel billboard across the street.

Then, suddenly, I had an idea. It wasn't a good idea, but it was my first one in just over eight chapters and beggars can't be choosers. I figured it this way: the Nifk dame knew who the Fat Man was. As long as she was hanging around Spike there was no way I was going to get any information out of her, mainly because Spike was bigger than me and I'm not crazy enough to tangle with guys who are bigger than me. So what I had to do was get the Nifk dame to see me alone. I wasn't certain, but I was pretty sure I could take her. Most dames I can take unless they're bigger than me or fight dirty. But how was I going to get her to see me alone? That one was easy: since she was a hooker, all I had to do was pretend I was an out-of-town businessman looking for a good time, call her up and tell her to meet me in some hotel room later that afternoon. It was so simple, I wondered why I hadn't thought of it before.

First I dialed the Astor Hotel and booked a room for noon. Then I dialed the Brass Knuckle Bar. The phone rang about five times before Spike finally picked up.

"Whosis?" he asked with all the charm of a sex-starved piranha.

"This here's Joe Bob Johnson," I said, disguising my voice with a Texan drawl. "Lemme speak to Olga."

I heard him drop the phone and call out for the Nifk dame. Ten seconds later, she picked up.

"Yeah?" she said.

"Howdy, gal," I said, continuing the charade. "This here's Joe Bob Johnson from down Texas way, here in old New York for a convention. A good friend of mine recommended you-all real highly. Said you knew how to give a guy a good time."

"Yeah?" she said. "What'd ya have in mind?"

"Sexual intercourse," I said.

"No kidding, Dick Tracy," she said. My heart sped up. Did she know I was a dick? "Anything in particular you want? Anything you want me to bring along?"

"Just the usual," I said. "Whips, chains, whipped cream . . ."

"Diet or regular?"

"Regular," I said.

"Anything else?"

I was at a loss, so I faked it. "An extra dress, size ten, a vibrator, a dildo and a jar of peanut butter."

"Smooth or chunky?"

"Chunky."

"Is that it?"

"That's it," I said.

"It'll cost ya a pretty penny," she said.

"That's cheap," I said. "I was expecting to spend about fifty bucks or so."

"What are you, some kind of wise guy?" she asked. "My price is a hundred clams."

"Cherrystones or littlenecks?"

"Look, buster, I ain't got time for cute banter," she said. "Two hundred bucks buys you a good time. A hundred and fifty buys you a so-so time and a hundred'll buy you a lousy time."

I thought it over for a few seconds.

"Well, what's it gonna be, sport?" she asked impatiently.

"A lousy time will have to do," I said. "I'm on a tight budget."

"Suit yourself, pal," she said. "Where and when?"

I started to give her the logistics when something odd happened. At first I thought she had sneezed, so I said "Gesundheit," but she must have thought *I'd* sneezed, because she said "Gesundheit," too. One of us had to have been the sneezer. Unless either the cops had bugged my phone or Spike was listening in on another line at the bar. Given the choice, I'd take the cops over Spike any day.

Whoever it was, I figured I'd find out soon enough. The Nifk dame hung up and I poured myself another tall glass of rye. I'd need the fortification for my afternoon rendezvous.

❏

I'd never actually *paid* for sex before (unless you count my ex-wife, who used to charge me ten bucks), so my tryst with the Nifk dame was going to be a first. I figured once she was in the room and the door was locked, I'd threaten her with my roscoe until she gave me the poop I needed about the Fat Man. I might even slap her around a little if she needed convincing. I was pretty desperate at this point, and I knew if I didn't get a decent lead sooner or later, the cops would nab the killer and, once again, I'd be out of work.

I got over to the hotel around noon, registered and went up to my room to wait. I'd told the Nifk dame to meet me there at twelve-thirty, but I wanted to get there first to check the place out. I put the DO NOT DISTURB sign on the outer doorknob, turned the radio up in case Nifk and I got into a tussle, and ordered a couple of cocktails from room service. Then I settled into an armchair by the window and waited, keeping my hand on my gat just in case.

At twelve-fifteen there was a knock on the door. With one hand on my roscoe, I opened it. It was the chambermaid.

"Me make up room, yes?" she asked in a Puerto Rican accent.

"No," I said, pointing to the sign on the doorknob. "Do not disturbo, *comprende?*"

"Sí," she said. "Me make up room now."

I shrugged and let her in. While she unmade the bed, then remade the bed, I sat there twiddling my thumbs. After about ten minutes, she left.

At twelve-thirty there was another knock on the door. I opened it only to find another chambermaid. Again I pointed to the DO NOT DISTURB sign, but it was no use. The bed underwent yet another pointless make-over while I sat there like a dolt watching.

Two more maids and a half hour later, I

was still sitting there watching the bed linen fly. I was starting to get annoyed. Just my luck, I thought disconsolately, to be the only guy in New York to ever get stood up by a hooker.

Between one-thirty and three I took a short nap, did the crossword puzzle, drank both cocktails, watched *The Dating Game* on TV and, just for the hell of it, tore the fresh linen off the bed so the next maid wouldn't be too disappointed. Naturally, once the bed was in real disarray, the maid service stopped.

By about three-fifteen I got tired of waiting and dialed the Brass Knuckle Bar to see what was keeping the Nifk dame. Spike answered the phone, so I went through the Joe Bob Johnson routine again and asked him if he knew where she was. His answer took me aback.

"She left about two hours ago," he said gruffly.

"Did she say where she was going?" I asked, just in case she had other plans prior to our rendezvous.

"The Astor Hotel," he said. "Say, are you a flatfoot or something?"

I hung up on the bastard and instinctively ran to the window which overlooked the street. I knew deep down in my gut exactly what I'd find down there, and it only took one quick glance to verify the hunch. Police squad cars filled the street and a couple of paramedics were loading a stretcher into an ambulance. It had to be Nifk. If I hadn't had the window closed, I probably would've heard the whole thing.

The big question was, who killed her? Whoever it was figured to be the one behind the rest of the murders. I eliminated Spike right off—if it had been him he wouldn't have stuck around the Brass Knuckle Bar, because the cops would be due there any minute. But if it wasn't Spike, who was it? Frank Templeton? Fast Eydie? The Mob?

It didn't take me long to put two and two together. I'd been going around in circles for days, but suddenly, in a flash of insight, I had a solid hunch. If I was right, it would explain everything. Still, it was a bit farfetched, so just to make sure I was on the right track I dialed a friend of mine at the Municipal Court Building and asked him to look up the name Sam Spade, Jr., and check for aliases and name changes. Two minutes later, he came back with the information I needed. My hunch had been right! Suddenly, all the elements in this cockamamie case came together. The pieces in the jigsaw puzzle all fell gorgeously into their places. Sam Spade, Jr., and the Fat Man were one and the same person! Maybe.

I would have sat there and congratulated myself, but I had to work fast. Now that I knew who the killer was, I also knew that the Hackensacker dame's life was in grave danger. I knew I had to save her—she owed me eight hundred bucks.

Trying to stay calm, I dialed her number. The sonovabitch phone rang about half a dozen times before she picked it up. Finally, I heard her voice. The killer hadn't gotten there yet.

"It's Mac," I said. "I know who the Fat Man is."

"Who is it?" she asked.

"I haven't got time to explain and you probably wouldn't believe me anyway," I said. "I want you to listen to me very carefully: Are all your doors and windows locked?"

"Yes, why?"

"Good," I said. "Keep them locked. Stay home. If you've got a heater, keep it near you."

"Keep it near me?" she asked. "It weighs about eight hundred pounds and it's in the cellar."

"Jesus," I said. "What is it, a howitzer?"

"No, it's a heater. A gas heater, I believe."

"I don't mean your heater heater," I said, "I mean a gun. A gat. A roscoe. A piece. Get the picture?"

"A gun!" she said. "Am I in some kind of danger, Mac?"

"Good guess," I said. "Listen, there's no time for chatter now, baby. Do like I said. I'll be there as soon as I can."

"Oh Mac," she said, suddenly realizing the gravity of her predicament. "I'm scared. I better call the police!"

"NO!" I shouted. "Don't call the police. Whatever you do, don't call the police! I'll be right there. Don't answer the door no matter what. Understood?"

"Understood."

"Good girl."

I hung up and dashed out of the hotel room.

❏

Racing like a bat out of hell, I tore down the hall and jumped into the first open elevator. I knew I didn't have a second to spare. The Hackensacker dame was living on borrowed time, and Mr. Death was about to foreclose on the mortgage and send her into probate. Sure she'd lied to me half a dozen times, sure she'd taken advantage of my trust, but I was in love with the dame anyway, and I knew deep down that if I didn't save her now, if I didn't get there fast enough to keep her from getting knocked off, she'd never pay me the eight hundred bucks she owed me.

I was out of that elevator the minute the doors popped open, jogging full speed ahead through the lobby, dodging anybody who got in my way, like a football player who's got an appointment with the end zone. I was a mere twenty yards away from making a touchdown when someone tripped me and I felt myself rocket head first into a wedding cake that three bellboys had been carrying through the lobby.

After wiping the frosting out of my face, I glared up at the owner of the offending foot and couldn't believe my eyes.

It was none other than my old nemesis, Detective O'Shaughnessy.

He was smiling complacently, as were the three beat cops to his left.

"You're under arrest, Slade," he said.

I picked myself up and dusted off my fedora. An old lady who was part of the wedding party looked at the decimated cake and kicked me in the shins. "For what?" I said belligerently.

"For the murder of Olga Nifk," O'Shaughnessy said.

"Forget it, O'Shaughnessy," I said. "I've been in a hotel room all afternoon. I got an iron-clad alibi and six Puerto Rican chambermaids who'll back me up."

"Sure," O'Shaughnessy said. "And I suppose the Pope is Catholic."

I didn't have time to argue with him. If he decided to be a bastard and take me in, I'd be sitting in the slammer for four hours while the killer was busy making sausage links out of the Hackensacker dame.

One of the beat cops reached for his handcuffs and came toward me. I knew I had to act fast or it would be all over. Instinctively, I pulled out my roscoe, grabbed the old lady who'd kicked me in the shins, and pointed the gat at her head.

"All right," I said to O'Shaughnessy. "One move and Whistler's Mother here gets an instant lobotomy."

"Take your hands off me, sonny!" the old bag said, struggling to get loose. "You're mussing my new hat!"

I moved the gun over a couple of inches so that it was away from the old dame's hat. When all of this was over, I didn't want to get a hat-blocking bill in the mail.

"Don't move, O'Shaughnessy," I said,

edging toward the revolving door, "and nobody'll get hurt."

"You'll do six years for this, Slade," O'Shaughnessy said. "I'll see to it personally. You hear me, Slade? Sing Sing!"

Why he wanted me to sing at that point I'll never know, but I didn't have time to think about it. I took the old lady through the revolving door with me and gently nudged her into my jalopy, which was parked on the street.

"Don't try and follow me, O'Shaughnessy," I said, pointing my gat at the old lady, "or Grandma here gets a one-way ticket to Palookasville."

"If you don't mind my saying so, young man," the old dame said, "I think you mean Forest Lawn, not Palookasville. Palookasville is where old boxers go."

"I'm in charge here, lady," I said. And with that I floored the gas pedal and we were out of there in a flash.

With one hand on the wheel and the other on my gat, I sped crosstown to the East River Drive and headed for Connecticut at a steady seventy miles per hour, weaving through the traffic like a professional race-car driver. I knew I didn't have a second to waste. If the killer got there before I did, the Hackensacker dame would be Swiss cheese on rye with a side of cole slaw. And if I failed to nab the killer, I'd be sent up the river for kidnapping or, in this case, geezernapping, since the old lady sitting next to me was certainly no kid.

While I drove, I explained to the old biddy why I'd had to take her hostage, that it had been a matter of life and death and so on. I didn't want her to think I did this kind of thing on a regular basis. She seemed to understand.

"Hell's bells, sonny," she said, "I haven't had this much excitement since I won the Pillsbury Bake-Off in 'twenty-six! Can't you get this heap to go any faster?"

I floored it, getting the speedometer up to eighty-five, and we tore past the landscape like a bullet.

We were there in twenty-five minutes. I parked my jalopy a couple of hundred yards from the Hackensacker estate just in case the killer hadn't gotten there yet, and told the old lady to sit tight.

"Sit tight my ass," she said. "It's not every day I get to see a private eye in action."

"Private dick," I corrected.

"Watch your language, young man," she said. "I'm coming with you and that's that. I wouldn't miss this for all the tea in China."

I sighed. "Look, lady," I said, "chances are, there's going to be some shooting going on and I don't want you catching a bullet."

"Who's going to throw a bullet at *me?*" she asked.

I sighed again, vowing to myself to be a little choosier the next time I had to take somebody hostage, maybe get a few references first.

"Look, lady," I said, as patiently as I could. "You've got two choices: either you stay put here on your own or I'll have to tie you to the car."

She thought it over for a second or two. "All right, young man," she said finally, "you talked me into it."

"Then you'll stay put?"

"Not a chance," she said. "I'm going for the second choice. Bondage."

I slapped my forehead in frustration. Of all the people in New York I *could* have taken hostage, *I* had to pick an eighty-five-year-old bondage freak.

Sighing, I opened the trunk and took out the few feet of rope I kept back there for tying people up. Keeping the knots fairly loose so as not to make them too painful, I tied the old biddy to the car door and started on my way.

"Hold your horses, buster," she said before I'd gotten more than ten feet away. "Aren't you forgetting something?"

"What?" I asked.

"The gag," she said. "You forgot the gag."

"I don't have a gag," I said. "They were out of gags the last time I went to the store."

"Then stuff a hanky or a bandana in my mouth or something," she said. "Either do the job right, young man, or don't do it at all."

At this point I was ready to go one step beyond gag and strangle the old witch, but I controlled myself, took out a clean handkerchief and stuffed it in her mouth, taking care not to jar her dentures too much. She nodded approval, and at last I was on my way.

It had already gotten dark and, since the grounds were badly lit, I darted in the shadows until I'd gotten to the front door. Relieved to see that the Hackensacker dame had followed my instructions and securely locked it, I rang the doorbell and waited. There was no answer. I rang again. Again, no answer. After three more answerless rings, I realized what the problem was— I'd told her not to let anyone in the house no matter what and she was following my instructions to the letter.

Somehow, though, I had to get in. Darting from shadow to shadow, I snuck to the side of the huge mansion and tried to pry open the first window I came to. It was bolted shut and the shade was drawn, yet I could make out that there was a night light on in the room.

"It's me," I whispered. "Open up."

But there was no answer from inside. This time I raised my voice a few decibels. "Dammit!" I shouted. "Let me in. It's Mac Slade!"

Finally the shade went up and I saw the Hackensacker dame at the window looking out.

"Down here," I said. "In the bushes."

She spotted me. "Oh Mac!" she said. "You'd better get out of there right away!"

"Why?" I asked.

I got my answer immediately in the form of a jet spray of water right smack in the area where the sun don't shine. Maybe the sun didn't shine there, but it sure rained a lot. Within seconds, the goddamn sprinklers had soaked me to the skin again.

Shaking her head apologetically, the Hackensacker dame opened the window, and I crawled inside, drops of water forming an instant puddle around my feet.

"Oh, I'm so sorry, Mac," she said. "It's on an automatic timer."

"Don't worry about it," I said. "I'm just

glad I got here in time. Are you all right, baby?"

"I'm fine, Mac," she said. "Just a little frightened."

I took her in my damp arms and kissed her deeply. In midsmooch, I heard a noise that seemed to be coming from the basement stairs.

"Shhhh," I said. "Did you hear that?"

She perked up her ears like a dalmation. "Yes," she said. "That's just Henry, my butler, and Perkins, my chauffeur, in the cellar."

"What are they doing in the cellar at this time of night?"

"Bringing the heater upstairs," she said. "Just like you said."

I breathed a sigh of relief and laughed.

"What's so funny, Mac?" she asked, her doelike eyes looking up at me innocently.

"Nothing, baby," I said. "I'm just relieved that you're all right, that's all."

"Oh, Mac," she said, cradling herself in my arms. "I was so scared after you called. I've never been so terrified in all my life."

"It's all right," I said, stroking her hair. "I'm here now. Nobody's going to hurt you."

"But you haven't told me who the killer is yet, Mac," she said.

"All in good time, baby," I said. "But first I sure could use a drink and a nice dry bathrobe."

❑

After drying up and wetting my whistle with a glass of expensive cognac, I explained the whole sordid story to her. The more I talked, the surer I was that my hunch was right.

"How did you ever figure it all out?" Brigitte Hackensacker asked when I'd finished explaining it to her. "It's so complex, so convoluted, so . . . incredibly contrived."

"That's the thing about murder mysteries," I said. "They're full of misleading clues, red herrings and suspicious implications, but somehow, toward the last chapter, all the loose ends miraculously come together."

"And you really think the killer is after me?"

"I'm afraid so," I said.

At that, the Hackensacker dame threw herself in my protective embrace. She was trembling like a bowl of Jell-O.

"Hold me, Mac," she said. "Just hold me tight and never let me go."

I did what she asked, though I knew that sooner or later I'd have to let her go— eventually one of us would have to go to the bathroom.

I raised her chin up and was about to plant a kiss on her yearning lips when I was interrupted by a voice. It was the unmistakable voice of the killer.

"Well, well, well," the killer said, pointing a gat at us, "isn't this a romantic little scenario."

"Hello, Fat Man," I said, looking the killer right in the eye. "Or should I call you Sam?"

"Hello, Mac," the killer said. "I never thought you'd ever get around to solving this one. Congratulations."

"It wasn't easy," I said. "You stuck in enough red herrings to feed a school of dolphins."

"Maybe I should've stuck in a few more," the killer continued. "What tipped you off that it was me all along?"

"The daffodils," I said. "I remembered you were allergic to daffodils. There was a sneeze over the phone when I called the Nifk dame, and at first I thought it was either the cops or Spike, but then I remembered your allergy."

"Clever," the killer said. "I should have been more careful. Taken an antihistamine."

"It wouldn't have made any difference," I said. "The daffodils were just confirmation. I already had a hunch it was you. You were the only one who could've taken those three bullets out of my gat, especially the one I found in the dummy, you were the only one who knew where I was most of the time, the only one who could've arranged things around my schedule. You even had your pal Spike take a shot at me in midtown to throw me off. The Frank Templeton connection threw me off for a while until I realized it was just a coincidence. What really confused me, though, was the Sam Spade, Jr., business. I couldn't figure how the cops could've gotten the name before I did."

"Simple," the killer said. "I tipped them off anonymously that Sam Spade would be the murderer's next victim just to throw them off. It worked. But you still haven't told me how you put the Fat Man and me together."

"Pure luck," I said. "One day while I was driving through town I saw a poster of a Broadway showgirl and it stuck in my mind. It wasn't until a couple of days later that I remembered that you'd originally come to town to break into show business and that you'd changed your name from Samantha Spade to Tuesday DeVere, and that after you'd given up on Broadway and come to work for me you'd decided to keep your stage name. The Fat Man business was pretty clever, too, but you knew that would confuse me even more because there are hundreds of Fat Men out there."

"Right so far," Tuesday said.

"Then you bumped the Nifk dame off when you found out that she and Spike were blackmailing the Hackensacker dame behind your back. You figured you couldn't trust her to keep her yap shut, so you nailed her before she was supposed to meet me this afternoon."

"Right again," Tuesday said.

"What I don't get is why you killed Hammer and Marlowe," I said.

"That was the whole point," Tuesday explained. "I was madly in love with you, Mac. It pained me to see you losing all your business to those two young dicks. I'd seen it break my father years ago, and I didn't want to see it break you. So I kidnapped Link Hackensacker, knowing that his sister would be rich and savvy enough to go to Hammer and Marlowe before knocking on your door. When Hammer and Marlowe got too close, I had Nifk and Spike bump them off and make it look like you'd done it. I knew the cops would clear you eventually."

"Why did you kill the Hackensacker kid?" I asked.

"I didn't," Tuesday said. "I had him hidden out in a cabin in the Catskills, but somehow he escaped and I guess the Mob goons finally found him. He was dead before I even knew about it. You believe me, don't you, Mac?"

"Sure, baby," I said. "So, basically, you did all of this for me?"

"Right."

"I'm touched, sweetheart," I said, "but if you were so concerned about my career, you could've just taken out a full-page ad somewhere. You didn't have to go to all this trouble."

"Oh Mac," she said, a stray tear rolling down her cheek. "It could've been so great, just you and me, solving cases together, going home together at night after a hard day at the office, raising a family. I didn't count on you falling for this bimbo."

"I resent that!" the Hackensacker dame said. I motioned for her to keep her yap shut.

"Is it too late for us, Mac?" Tuesday cried, another tear finding its way down her cheek.

"I'm afraid so, Tuesday," I said. "Even if I wanted to take up with you, I couldn't.

I'm a dick and you're a murderer. At the very least, it'd be a conflict of interest."

Tuesday was weeping full blast now. "You don't have to turn me in," she said. "If you love me at all, Mac, you won't turn me in."

"Forget it, baby," I said. "I'm up to my ears in this thing. O'Shaughnessy's got me on a kidnapping rap. If I don't cough up the murderer, I'm done for. It's you or me, babe, and if you think I'm going to take a fall to keep your hide out of the slammer, you're crazy."

"Well, there's no reason to get testy about it," she said. "I was only asking."

"Now be a good girl, Tuesday, and hand over that roscoe," I said as gently as I could.

But she only firmed up her grip on it. "No way, José," she said. "The way I see it I've got two choices here—either I bump both of you off or I get to spend the rest of my life in the slammer. Now, what kind of choice is that?"

"Depends on how you look at it," I said. "From where I'm standing, I'd recommend the slammer."

Tuesday shook her head, definitely not a good sign. "I have nothing to live for," she said. "You're in love with this . . . this . . . tramp."

"I've taken just about enough of these insults," the Hackensacker dame said. "I refuse to be insulted by someone who is a guest in my house! I won't stand here and take this lying down."

"Look at it this way, Tuesday," I said, nudging the Hackensacker dame in the ribs. "You've only murdered three people and kidnapped a fourth. The way things are nowadays, you'll be out on parole in six months."

But she only shook her head. "Oh Mac," she said, "I only came out here to knock *her* off. I was jealous. I didn't want to have to harm you. Of all the cases you've had, why did you have to solve this one?"

"Law of averages?" I opined.

"Don't you see, Mac?" she cried. "I have to kill you too. You don't love me anyway, and even if you didn't turn me in I doubt if you'd want to keep me on your payroll."

There was a fire in her eyes that said she meant every word. I knew I had to do something and quick, otherwise we'd both be fertilizing the ragweed out at Forest Lawn. Slowly, I moved my hand toward my gat, which I'd stowed in the pocket of my bathrobe just in case. It wasn't there.

The Hackensacker dame saw me go for it, and a guilty look came over her gorgeous face.

"Sorry, Mac," she said. "I put it in the dryer with your clothes."

"Nice going," I said.

Meanwhile, Tuesday had raised her roscoe toward my head. "All right," she said, closing her eyes to squeeze out the tears. "Who wants it first?"

I looked at the Hackensacker dame and she looked at me, terror lighting up her eyes. "Age before beauty," she said.

"Ladies first," I said. "I insist."

"You picked a fine time to suddenly become a gentleman," she said.

"All right," I said. "I'll choose you for it." We both curled our fingers and raised our arms. "Once, twice, three, shoot," I said. One for her. "Once, twice, three, shoot," I repeated. One for me. "Once, twice, three, shoot."

She won.

"Okay, Tuesday," I said, closing my eyes. "I'm ready. Pull the lousy trigger and make it fast. And aim carefully. I can't afford a hospital visit."

I peeked out from under my half-closed lids and saw Tuesday trying to steady her shaking hand. She cocked the gun. She was ready.

Just then, the door crashed open, Tuesday tumbled forward with a lurch and the gun exploded. It had all happened so fast, for a second I didn't know whether I was still alive or dead.

When the smoke from Tuesday's spent revolver cleared, I saw the prettiest sight I'd seen in years.

"Don't just stand there with a dumb look on your kisser, sonny," my octogenarian hostage said, wielding her oversized handbag. "Get the dame's roscoe."

I grabbed Tuesday's gat off the floor and held it steady on her as she got up.

"Nice work, lady," I said to the old dame who'd just saved my life. "You got here in the nick of time."

"No kidding, Dick Tracy," she said. "And if you ask me, sonny, you could use a refresher course in Elementary Tying and Gagging. A retarded Boy Scout could've tied a better knot."

I let the remark pass. The Hackensacker dame, who'd been standing in the corner frozen with fear ever since the gat had gone off, came over to me and burrowed her trembling body under my free arm, hugging me so tightly I thought I was going to pee in my pants.

"Oh Mac," she said. "Thank God it's all over. Now we can take up where we left off."

"I'm afraid not, baby," I said. "Not unless you can give me a good reason why you paid to have your own brother bumped off."

"Oh Mac, don't play games with me," she said. "I've been through a lot. How can you joke at a time like this?"

"I'm through playing the sap for you, baby," I said. "I've played the sap long enough and things are starting to get a little too sticky for yours truly."

Her eyes told me that she knew the game was over and that she'd lost.

"How did you know?" she asked finally.

"I didn't," I said. "Not until you just verified it. I didn't have a clue and all along I thought Tuesday did it, but why should she lie after confessing to the other murders? It was just a wild guess really. Though one thing did bother me."

"I'm listening," she said none too friendly.

"That day we met at Mamma Linguine's, I had a suspicion you'd been there before, and that you already knew Guido. Guilt was written all over your face."

"I know," she said. "I'd run out of notepaper."

"Let me guess at your motive," I said. "You wanted Link out of the way because he knew you'd killed your husband for the insurance money and he was blackmailing you to pay off his gambling debts for him. When Link disappeared, you went to Hammer, Marlowe and then me to find him so you could set him up. Besides, we provided the perfect cover for you, as did Olga Nifk's blackmailing scheme. You figured as long as you had hired three dicks and were paying extortion money to save your brother, no one would ever suspect you. But when Link escaped from Tuesday's cabin in the Catskills, he called you to pick him up and you called your friend Guido. The Hammer and Marlowe murders weren't part of your plan, but they worked in your favor by providing even

171

more cover, since you knew I'd figure that whoever killed the two dicks killed Link as well."

"Oh Mac," she cried desperately, "you won't turn me over to the police, will you? If you truly love me you won't. We can still be happy together. You still love me, don't you, Mac?"

"Maybe I do and maybe I don't," I said. "But the fact is, baby, we could never be happy together. Not as long as I knew you were a killer. And let's face it, that would be pretty hard to forget, even for me."

"You can't mean it, Mac," she said. "How can you let a little thing like murder stand in the way of our happiness?" She raised her gorgeous face to mine and gazed up at me with those beautiful doelike peepers. She could be pretty convincing.

"Then who's going to take the fall for your brother's murder?" I asked her.

Without a word, Brigitte Hackensacker let her gaze fall on Tuesday, who had been crying in the corner.

"She was going to kill both of us, Mac," the Hackensacker dame said. "Don't forget that. Plus she's already got three murders under her belt. What's another one more or less?"

I didn't have time to respond. Just then

the door flew open again, and this time O'Shaughnessy and half the New York Police Department barged in, guns drawn.

"Everybody freeze!" O'Shaughnessy shouted. We all obeyed and held our positions like a bunch of marble statues.

"I'm throwing the book at you, Slade," O'Shaughnessy said, pulling a volume out of a nearby bookshelf and hurling it across the room at me. I ducked in the nick of time, and the book, an abridged version of *The Decline and Fall of the Roman Empire,* sailed through a window.

"I hate to disappoint you, young man," my ex-hostage said to O'Shaughnessy, "but I do not intend to press charges against Mr. Slade. He's been very nice."

O'Shaughnessy was clearly crestfallen that he wasn't going to get me on a kidnapping rap. Just when he thought he'd aced me out, too. I almost felt sorry for the poor sap.

"Speeding, then," he said desperately. "You're under arrest for speeding. You were doing at least seventy through midtown."

I ignored him. "I got a present for you and your pal the D.A.," I said, nodding toward Tuesday. "The Hardboiled Dicks' Killer in the flesh."

"Her!" O'Shaughnessy said, clearly taken aback. "Your own gal Friday, Tuesday?"

"That's right," I said. "She killed Hammer and Marlowe, kidnapped Link Hackensacker and bumped off the Nifk dame. You can round up her only living accomplice at a joint called the Brass Knuckle Bar in Times Square—the barkeep, a Viking impersonator named Spike. You can't miss the mug. And while you're at it, you can collar Guido Provolone for murder, too."

"You mean Murder One," the old lady corrected.

"Murder One too," I said. "Too as in also."

O'Shaughnessy sighed and ordered one of his uniformed flunkies to handcuff Tuesday and take her out to the paddy wagon. I could tell he was confused.

"This better wash, Slade," he said threateningly.

"It'll wash," I assured him. "It won't spin-dry, but it'll wash."

"And what about the Hackensacker kid?" he asked suddenly. "She nail him too?"

Brigitte Hackensacker turned those gorgeous eyes on me and gave me a look that

I'll never forget as long as I live. I swallowed hard, but I couldn't get the words out. Sure, I was in love with her, as in love with anyone as a mug like me is likely to ever get, but what kind of life would it be married to a dame who'd had her own brother strangled by the Mob? Anybody who'd kill a relative is not a safe bet for matrimony. What would stop her from bumping off an uncle or an aunt or a niece or even a husband? In-laws would be doomed from the start. With only me standing between her and the slammer, how could I ever know if she really loved me or if she was just playing for time? Sure, we could be happy for a while, but one day I'd wake up with an ice pick in my head.

Without a word, I peeled her arms off of me and handed her over to O'Shaughnessy.

"I'm sorry it had to end this way, baby," I said trying to fight the tears that were forming in my eyes, "and if it'll make you feel any better, I'll be happy to forget about the $801.98 you still owe me."

She didn't say anything. Not even so much as a so long. She just stared straight ahead with no expression in her eyes as the cops snapped on the cuffs and led her out to the paddy wagon. I watched as she hiked her dress up a few crucial inches before climbing in. One thing was for sure—the dame had a set of gams that just wouldn't quit, not even on Palm Sunday.